While
SNOWBOUND

BOOKS BY ANNA J. MCINTYRE

COULSON'S WIFE

COULSON'S CRUCIBLE

COULSON'S LESSONS

COULSON'S SECRET

COULSON'S RECKONING

UNLOCKED ♥ HEARTS

SUNDERED HEARTS

AFTER SUNDOWN

WHILE SNOWBOUND

SUGAR RUSH

While SNOWBOUND

Anna J. McIntyre

While Snowbound
By Anna J. McIntyre
(Unlocked Hearts Series)
A Novel
By Anna J. McIntyre
Cover Design: Elizabeth Mackey
Editor: Suzie O'Connell

This novel is a work of fiction.
Any resemblance to places or actual persons,
living or dead is entirely coincidental.
www.robeth.com

ISBN: 978-1-949977-46-2

To Elizabeth, for always being my champion. This adventure wouldn't be half as much fun without you by my side. Thank you for the never ending support, beautiful covers that capture the spirit of my stories, and for being the best daughter a mother could ever hope for. You make me proud every day.

CHAPTER ONE

"Get that woman out of my bed!" Brady Gates shouted.

Those who knew him and heard the command understood he was pissed. Discovering a nude and shapely blonde sprawled provocatively atop the sheets in his hotel suite did not make Brady happy. The uninvited guest had pulled down the top coverlet of the freshly made bed before climbing in and waiting for his arrival.

Brady's displeasure did not deter her. Leaning back on the pile of pillows along the headboard, she parted her thighs slightly, giving him a clear view of what she offered. Sliding her right hand down her inner thigh, her smile wavered, perplexed at his reaction.

Brady had entered his hotel suite alone, leaving

his entourage lingering in the hallway, still engaged in some debate over a recent sports game. Since the band and crew were occupying the entire floor of the hotel, there was no reason to be overly concerned about disturbing other hotel guests.

After entering the suite, he went straight through the living area to the bedroom, en route to the bathroom. Upon entering, he left the door leading to the hallway ajar. Brady never shared a hotel room with other members of his band or crew, yet his main bodyguard and personal assistant, Kevin Jones, always stayed in the adjoining room.

How she managed to get into the private hotel suite could be explained by the silly grin now plastered on the bellboy, who was too busy thinking of the recent hand job the hot blonde stranger had given him, to focus on the real possibility that he might lose his job over his recent indiscretion.

Her intent was clear. She, like countless women before her, wanted to have sex with the famous rock star. It didn't matter to her that she had never met Brady Gates, or that they had never exchanged any correspondence. She had every confidence that once Brady found her willing and ready, he would climb on top and give her a ride to remember. After all, she had placed first in several local beauty contests, and just last week, won a hundred bucks in a wet T-shirt contest at her favorite pub.

Kevin, who was still standing in the hallway

talking to several band members, responded immediately. After shouting, Brady stepped back into the living area of the suite and watched dispassionately as Kevin and several of the other bodyguards rushed past him and into the bedroom area. While pulling the intruder from the bed, one of the bodyguards ripped the top sheet from the mattress and tossed it around the woman before hauling her from the room.

"Get your fucking hands off me!" she screeched, no longer the coy and accommodating creature who'd been lounging uninvited on the musician's bed just moments earlier. Brady calmly picked up the telephone in his hotel suite and called downstairs to hotel management as he watched the men evict his uninvited guest. He suspected by the time they reached the elevator they would be greeted by hotel security.

When Kevin first started working for Brady Gates three years earlier, he had wondered briefly if the rock star was gay. After all, why else would a healthy, heterosexual male have a problem with beautiful women showing up in his dressing room or hotel suite? Of course, not all the women were gorgeous. He had to admit some looked well used, and with those, he understood his employer's objection. Wisely, he chose not to question Brady, especially considering the job paid extremely well. After a few months, Kevin understood the problem: even a seem ingly good thing gets tedious and annoying if excessive.

It became especially sensitive when the overly amorous groupie was underage. This was one reason Brady chose to be surrounded by his trusted entourage, giving any wayward teen little chance to be alone in a compromising situation with the famous star. Brady was determined to avoid the trap of a calculating bitch looking for an opportunity to exploit him for financial gain.

Since obtaining fame, Brady Gates had never engaged in sex with groupies. He frequently enjoyed the company of A-list socialites and stars. His only rule regarding sex—he chose his partners, and they weren't random strangers who showed up in his bed or dressing room.

Just twenty-eight years of age, Brady Gates was used to having any woman he wanted. While he never pursued married women, he was confident in his ability to easily bring one into his bed, if that were his desire.

He had never been naïve and was fully aware of the dangers of unprotected sex and sex with multiple partners, so he was discrete, and always wore a condom. Unlike many of his fellow rockers, Brady never experimented with drugs, and while he enjoyed beer, he rarely became intoxicated. His state of constant sobriety prevented him from waking up in some stranger's bed.

Kevin found Brady sitting at the bar in the living room section of the rock star's hotel suite when he returned fifteen minutes later. Brady hadn't changed his clothes and was still wearing black denims with a black silk, long-sleeved shirt tucked into the belted waistband of his tight-fitting pants. He'd kicked off his shoes and socks and sat on a barstool, drinking a bottle of imported beer as he rested his elbows casually against the marble bar top.

Brady was obviously agitated. Unruly fans were a common annoyance, and typically, he brushed off the inconvenience and let his employees handle the situation. The uninvited nude blonde was not the primary source of his dark mood; it was just the incident that sent him over the edge.

"They're sending up housekeeping to change the sheets," Kevin explained as he grabbed a beer from the courtesy bar and sat at the barstool next to his employer.

Brady just nodded in response to the clean sheets. He didn't ask where the rest of the crew went, assuming they had all gone back to their own rooms. He didn't ask what happened to the nude girl. He didn't care.

"I can't work like this, Kev," Brady said, downing the last of his beer. "I need to focus on my writing, and I can't do that when groupies keep showing up in my bed."

"You want to change hotels?"

"Why? We'll just have the same problem. And no offense, but I want some space. I need to be alone."

"And who'll drag the women from your bed?" Kevin was only half-teasing.

"I need to get away for a while. Alone. But not sure how to do that anymore. I need to find a nice, quiet place, where I can think, work on some songs, and not have to deal with all this bullshit." Brady set his empty bottle on the bar top. Exasperated, he combed his fingers through his dark hair.

The two men sat in silence for a few minutes, each pondering Brady's current dilemma and how it might be resolved.

During the past five years, Brady had been living a nomadic life, moving from one luxury hotel suite to another with his band and crew. He'd considered purchasing a house, so he would have somewhere to go when he wanted to be alone, like now. Yet, he never seemed to find the time to shop real estate or employ a suitable Realtor.

"I've an idea. How about you hide out for a few weeks at a nice, remote mountain cabin. Of course, you'll have to cook for yourself, and you won't have maid service, but I imagine you'd be willing to sacrifice that in exchange for some privacy."

"Where, exactly, do I find such a cabin without tipping off the paparazzi?" Brady stood up and walked around the bar to grab another beer from the small refrigerator.

"I've a cousin who rents out cabins up in Shipley Mountain. There's no snow skiing up there, so renters tend to be summer visitors who take advantage of the lake. During the winter, the lake freezes over and they close up the rentals. But I'm sure she'll agree to rent you one."

"Can we trust her to keep quiet?"

"Yes," Kevin assured him, but decided not to mention that his cousin was a fan and would probably be as goofy as some of Brady's groupies if she wasn't already happily married and six months pregnant. "Of course, you'll need to take a four-wheel drive up there. I don't think they have snow yet, but being November, it can come at any time. You can use my Jeep, if you want."

"I guess the crew can camp out here for a few more days, let people think I'm still at the hotel. Go ahead and make arrangements, but let's keep this between you and me. I'd prefer the crew not know where I'm going, and if possible, I'd like them to assume I'm still here."

"I don't think that'll be a problem. How long do you want me to rent the cabin for?"

"I'd like it for the rest of the month. I don't know if I'll stay that long. That gives us December to work on the new songs for the New Year's concert."

"You want to stay through Thanksgiving? Alone?"

"Thanksgiving's just another day for me. Plus,

this will give the crew the chance to get home for the holiday. Let me think about it, how I want to handle this. You go call your cousin, and I'll figure out what to say to everyone."

"OH, MY GAWD! BRADY GATES... AT ONE OF OUR cabins!" Amanda fairly squealed into the phone. She closed her eyes and envisioned the famous rock star. Last year, Kevin had given her concert tickets, but she was disappointed when he wasn't able to introduce her to Gates.

Brady Gates was not only one of the hottest commodities in the rock world; he had been voted sexiest man of the year—*twice*. She once asked her cousin if Brady wore tinted contact lenses, since his eyes were such a striking shade of sapphire blue. Kevin only responded with, "Don't be lame. They're just blue eyes." It left her wondering if the photographs of Brady were tinted to bring out the extraordinary color, which would account for her cousin's comment that they were *just blue eyes*. Maybe they were, in person. But since she had never seen him up close, she had no way of knowing.

He was about her cousin's height, standing just under six feet, and appeared very athletic and fit, as if he worked out on a regular basis. She imagined all that dancing around on stage kept him fit. He wasn't scrawny, but neither did he have a bulky physique.

"Well, not if anyone's standing with you in your office and just heard that outburst," Kevin said with mild disgust as he shook his head. Alone in his hotel room, he looked out the window as he spoke to his cousin on the cell phone.

"No, no, I'm alone. But can I tell Chad, please?"

"Do you always tell your husband details about your tenants?"

"No, you know he isn't involved with the rental business."

"Then please, Mandy, this once, don't say anything to Chad until December. Or we won't rent the cabin."

"Gee, you don't trust Chad?" Amanda asked with a pout.

"It's not a matter of trust. But you tell Chad, then he mentions it to someone he thinks he can trust to keep a secret—and then that person does the same, and the next thing we know, we have paparazzi and horny groupies crawling all over the mountain."

"You know, they're predicting snow this week. I imagine it will keep the paparazzi at bay."

"Trust me, cuz, not when Brady Gates is the target. Come on, do we have a deal? Will you rent me a cabin and keep it secret? You can tell the world in December. Of course, if Brady likes the cabin, he might return next winter, if his secret retreat remains a secret."

"Oh, that would be so cool!" Amanda said excitedly. "Yes, Kevin, I promise. I won't say anything to Chad. I'll give you the Cooper Cabin. Unlike some of my owners who use their cabins during the holidays, I know the Coopers aren't able to come up this winter and will be thrilled to have a renter. They don't have to know who I rented it to. But I'll need to get up there and check on the firewood, and give the cabin a good cleaning."

"If you're going up there anyway, can I get you to stock the place with supplies, groceries?"

"Sure, no problem. I'll even put fresh sheets on the bed and wash the towels, so they aren't all musty."

"You do that for all your guests?" Kevin asked with a laugh.

"No, but we are talking about Brady Gates! Normally, tenants are responsible for putting their own sheets on the bed, and washing linens and towels."

"I'll send you a grocery list, and some money to cover the expenses. Can you get everything done by Friday?"

"No problem. I'll have the cabin in order, for your boss before the weekend."

KEVIN'S BUILD WAS SIMILAR TO THE ROCK STAR, MAKING it easy for him to purchase clothes for Brady's mountain trip. When asked why he was buying all the winter gear, Kevin fabricated a tale about a Christmas ski trip. Instead of taking the packages directly to Brady, he brought them to his own room and used the interior adjoining door to enter his boss' suite.

Just twenty-four hours had passed since dragging the naked woman from Brady's hotel suite, and already Kevin had booked the cabin and purchased clothes for his employer. Brady was anxious to be on his way. The idea of spending the rest of the month at an isolated mountain cabin was very appealing. He could not remember the last time he had been alone, without some bodyguard, roadie or groupie underfoot.

That evening, Brady met with his road crew to make the announcement.

"I need to focus on my writing, and I'm having a difficult time doing it with all these distractions. I need to finish before December if we're going to introduce the songs at the New Year's concert," Brady explained. "I don't want to be disturbed. Kevin will be bringing me meals over the next few weeks. I don't want any of you to freak if I don't leave my room for the rest of the month. All I ask is that you keep the damn groupies away from me, and help Kevin do his job. I see no reason why most of you can't take some time off now and visit your families. Kevin has already agreed to help me out, so you guys coordinate this with him. Since I plan to stay close to my room, I don't see security as a significant issue."

CHAPTER TWO

"I have to tell you a secret, or I'm going to burst!" Amanda said excitedly the moment Ella Lewis walked into the rental office.

"Well, we wouldn't want you to burst. That would be messy." Ella chuckled. She gave her friend a welcoming hug after closing the door behind her, shutting out the frigid November day. The two friends stood in the middle of the office as Amanda hopped up and down excitedly, reminding Ella of a child who needed to visit the bathroom. Considering Amanda's state of pregnancy, it was entirely possible that was the reason for her hopping about.

The rental office was situated at the base of Shipley Mountain in the quaint village with the same name. It was a traditional log cabin, not a pre-fab structure, and well over fifty years old. Braided throw rugs covered its wood floors, and a raging fire in the stone fireplace along the far wall provided heat. Although it was clean and dust free, it had never been updated or refurbished. The office furniture consisted of an oak roll top desk - a reproduction - and three oak file cabinets pushed along one wall, also reproductions. A vintage brass coat rack stood near the door, and a couch faced the fireplace.

"But you must promise not to tell anyone!" Amanda insisted, still hopping a bit. Ella pulled off her gloves and stuffed them in her coat pocket. She then removed the coat and hung it on the brass rack before turning to face her friend.

"You know, the best way to keep a secret is to not share it," Ella reminded Amanda, her eyes twinkling. She knew full well Amanda would probably burst if she refused to listen.

"I can't tell Chad, but I will absolutely die if I don't tell someone! And I know I can trust you. You never tell secrets!"

"You're keeping something from Chad? My, this is starting to sound interesting," Ella said as she sat on the small couch, enjoying the warmth emanating from the fireplace. Instead of joining her friend on the sofa, Amanda stood before the fireplace and faced Ella. Both young women were dressed similarly, clad in denims, boots, and bulky pullover sweaters. Amanda's prominent baby bump pushed out the front of her sweater.

Amanda's hazel eyes swept over her friend's face.

Ella's clear complexion was slightly flushed from the brisk November air, and it looked as if the only makeup she wore was a light pink gloss on her full lips. Blessed with naturally dark and curly lashes, there was no reason for Ella to wear mascara. Her hair fell just past her shoulders and flipped up at the ends. Naturally mousy brown, she had added blonde highlights that complimented her complexion. While she didn't use an eyebrow pencil, her beautician shaped her brows, so they arched gracefully over her large blue-green eyes.

"I promised my cousin I wouldn't tell Chad. Actually, I'm not supposed to tell anyone," Amanda admitted, no longer hopping about excitedly.

"Okay, I won't tell anyone," Ella vowed, waiting to hear what her friend had to say.

"I've rented out one of the cabins for the rest of November."

"I sure hope it isn't mine! You knew I was coming to pick up the keys." Ella frowned. "I didn't think you normally did winter rentals."

"No, it isn't yours. I've rented out the Cooper Cabin. I already cleared it with them."

"Then why do you say it's some secret? Obviously the Coopers know."

"The secret isn't that I rented a cabin for November, but who I rented it to!"

"Okay, who is the renter?"

"Brady Gates!" Amanda excitedly exclaimed,

then remained quiet, waiting for her friend's reaction. Instead of showing any emotion, Ella just frowned.

"Brady Gates? Am I supposed to know who that is?"

"Oh, come on Ella, Brady Gates! You have to know who that is!" Amanda stomped one foot impatiently, waiting for her friend to show a proper response. Ella thought a moment and then shook her head.

"Sorry, I haven't a clue."

"Aw, come on Ella, everyone on this planet knows who Brady Gates is! He was voted sexiest man of the year! Twice!"

Ella shook her head. "Sorry, I never pay attention to that kinda stuff. Is he an actor or something?"

"No, he's a rock star. A very hot rock star," Amanda explained, staring dreamily into blank space.

"Is that anyway for a pregnant woman to behave?" Ella teased.

Amanda just giggled and patted her extended belly. "Oh, come on Ella, you have to know who he is." Amanda began singing one of Brady's songs, selecting one that was currently at the top of the charts. While a bit off key, Ella immediately recognized the tune.

"Oh, him. I hate his music," Ella said, interrupting the song.

"Seriously?"

"Seriously. Sorry, hard rock is not my thing. You know that. I'm a country girl. But if it makes you feel any better, if you asked me to name my favorite country singers, I'd have a difficult time recalling who sang what. I never remember names. I just know what I like when I hear it."

"I still can't believe you didn't know who he is. How can you be a writer and not know about this stuff?"

"What does writing historical romance have to do with knowing the names of current celebrities? They're just people, Amanda. So why the big secret about this Brady guy renting one of the cabins?"

"According to my cousin, he needs to get away from his fans and the paparazzi. I can't let anyone know he's going to be up there, because I can't risk someone bothering him. He's continually hounded by women."

"That poor guy!" Ella laughed sarcastically, and then added with sincerity, "Well your secret's safe with me. How about those cabin keys now?" Ella stood up.

"What happen to your set? Did you lose them again?"

"I just put them in a very safe place. Exactly where, I can't recall."

"Are you really going to your cabin this time of the year?"

"Hey, if it's good enough for your rock star, why not me?"

"Seriously, Ella, I hear they're expecting a big storm."

"Well, maybe you should worry more about your rock star renter than me. I know these mountains. Anyway, I need to finish my book and I keep letting the distractions get in the way. I figure without any Internet or television, I won't wander away from my manuscript."

"When are you planning to head up there?" Amanda asked as she walked over to her desk and started rummaging through a box of keys.

"I'll be heading up in the morning."

"I haven't rented your cabin since September; that was the last time I had it cleaned." Amanda found the set of keys she was looking for, and handed them to Ella.

"Remember, I was up there last month; it's fine. In fact, I suspect I may have left my set of keys sitting on the kitchen counter, now that I think about it."

"It's too bad your cabin isn't closer to the Coopers'; then you could check out Brady Gates and tell me how he looks in person."

"Aren't you going to meet him?"

"No. Remember, my cousin Kevin works for him."

"Now that you mention it, I think I remember you telling me that before."

"That was the concert I went to last year."

"That's right. So is Kevin picking up the keys for him?"

"No, Kevin instructed me to leave the keys under a rock outside the front door of the cabin. Brady is driving directly to the cabin, and when he leaves, he'll leave the key where he found it. I went up yesterday and stocked the pantry and refrigerator with enough supplies for three weeks. There was already firewood, so that wasn't an issue."

"I didn't know you did the full concierge service thing." Ella tucked the cabin keys in her purse.

"Ha, ha," Amanda said dryly. "Brady Gates is special."

"I guess he is!" Ella laughed. "Do me a favor and don't share your secret with anyone else. If this guy is as famous as you seem to think, the last thing I want is a bunch of stalkers crawling all over the mountain hunting for your guy. I'm looking forward to quiet."

"How long are you planning to stay?"

"Through November," Ella explained as she removed her jacket from the brass coat rack and slipped it on.

"You won't be home for Thanksgiving?"

"I consider the cabin home. Anyway, Mom and Dad are spending the holiday with my sister in California. I intend to make myself a nice Cornish game hen, in lieu of a turkey."

"Can't you stick around? Maybe we could grab lunch."

"I'd love to, but I need to pick up my groceries and finish packing. I imagine when I see you again in a few weeks that tummy of yours will be ready to pop!" Ella patted her friend's belly.

"Oh, I have another three months," Amanda groaned.

"Any other renters up on the mountain?" Ella asked as she reached for the doorknob.

"No. I imagine some of the owners might go up to their cabins for Thanksgiving, but none have called me yet to let me know—except you."

The two old friends chatted a few minutes longer before saying their goodbyes. Ella opened the door to the cabin office and stepped out onto the sidewalk. Greeted with a gust of frigid cold air, she hastily removed her gloves from the coat pocket and slipped them on her hands.

A few moments later, she climbed into her Suburban and headed for home. It was a forty-five minute drive from the village at Shipley Mountain to her condominium in Canyon City. It was one of the few condominiums in the area that allowed dogs the size of her Sam, who weighed in around sixty pounds. While Australian shepherds are normally high energy, Sam was her special needs dog that was unable to jump on the bed or into the Suburban without assistance.

Instead of going directly to her condominium to pack, she stopped at the grocery store. She considered briefly doing her shopping in the morning, before heading to the cabin, but didn't want to leave Sam alone in the car while in the store. Before leaving that day, she'd tossed several ice chests in the back of the Suburban, to hold the food that needed refrigeration.

She was annoyed with herself for misplacing the cabin keys, forcing her to take the trip up to the rental office to pick up a spare. She and Amanda had grown up together, and both their families owned cabins on Shipley Mountain. After Amanda married, she and her husband moved up to the village of Shipley, where Amanda's husband worked for the local fire department. Amanda got her real estate license and eventually started a vacation rental business, catering to summer visitors. Many of the cabin owners took advantage of the opportunity to earn a little additional income from their vacation homes.

Ella forgot the rule about never shopping when hungry, so she ended up purchasing far more groceries than were necessary for just one person. She stocked up on all her favorite holiday foods and indulged in the gourmet food section. It wasn't until she was loading the groceries from the shopping cart to the back of the Suburban that she began to question the wisdom of her purchase. She filled the ice chests with perishables, and placed the other items in the back of the car. She wondered briefly, where she would put her luggage and Sam, yet wasn't overly concerned, considering the size of the vehicle.

When she returned to her condominium, the first order of business was taking Sam for a walk. She intended to leave the groceries in her car, as the evenings had been in the low forties and the perishables were on ice. Sam was happy to see her mistress, and as was her custom, she didn't jump on Ella, but pushed the woman's denim covered thighs with a wet nose and gave little nibbles while letting out a howl or two, scolding Ella for being gone so long.

Ella gave Sam's furry back a rough brushing with her hand, and grabbed the leash from a hook by the front door. After slipping the collar around the dog's neck, the two stepped outside to take a walk.

When they returned twenty minutes later, Ella fed Sam and then made herself a sandwich before packing for her trip. She no longer left personal items at the cabin, since it was periodically used as a rental. Long ago, she made a packing list for the cabin, which she always referred to when going for a visit.

One item on the list was *portable typewriter*, and another, *typing paper*. When going to the cabin to write, Ella always took along an old portable typewriter and typing paper. The typewriter once belonged to her grandfather. So far, she had never had to use them at the cabin. But she wanted to be prepared, just in case the electricity went out and she couldn't use her laptop.

In her bathroom, she gathered up the items that she needed to pack. One was her packet of birth control pills. She held the package in her hand briefly and looked at it with a frown. In some ways, she thought it was foolish to keep taking the pill, as it had been almost a month since she'd broken up with her boyfriend, and she hadn't had sex since then.

"What I need more than these are my vibrator," Ella said aloud and let out a dry, sardonic laugh. Unlike many of her friends, she had never indulged in casual sex. As a precaution, she grabbed a box of tampons. She knew she wouldn't need them as she just finished her period and the pill kept her regular, but she figured it wouldn't hurt to take them along.

When she finished packing, she took a shower and slipped on her robe. Sitting on her living room couch with Sam by her feet on the floor, she grabbed her laptop from the coffee table. Balancing the computer on her lap, she turned it on.

Remembering what Amanda had said about the rock star, Ella decided to Google Brady Gates, curious to see if she would recognize him. A few clicks later, Ella landed on Brady's Wikipedia page. She stared at his picture, and wrinkled her nose a bit.

In the photograph, he was shirtless and wore white and black makeup on his chest and face. His features, contorted in an unattractive snarl and he held an electric guitar in his hands. The picture was obviously taken at a concert. Ella cringed at the sight.

"Yuck," she said aloud. Curious about the man, she did a second search, this one for images of Brady Gates. She scrolled through the photographs.

Ella conceded that without the unattractive makeup he was a handsome guy. The color of his eyes was quite startling, causing Ella to linger a bit over one picture. By the number of photographs of Brady with different women on his arm, he was obviously a player. While she was never good at remembering the names of movie stars, she recognized a number of notable female celebs, each holding possessively onto his arm.

According to his bio, he had never been married, and from what she could see, he didn't have a steady girlfriend. Yet, by the photographs, it was obvious he enjoyed an active social life.

"Oh, you poor baby," Ella said sarcastically when she recalled what Amanda had said about Brady needing to get away. "All those demanding women must really put a toll on you!" She laughed again and then closed the webpage, surfing to other topics that she found more interesting. Celebrity fodder never held Ella's interest for long. She found it all very boring.

CHAPTER THREE

*B*rady failed to notice the Suburban waiting to pull up to the fuel pump when he stepped on the gas and cut the larger vehicle off. He heard the screech of tires and the horn honk that followed. Glancing up into the rearview mirror, he saw the angry face of the other driver. Instead of feeling guilt, he was relieved she hadn't run into Kevin's Jeep. He wasn't concerned over hurting someone else's property—he could easily pay for that —but an accident would bring unwanted attention to himself and possibly interfere with his plans.

Brady shrugged disinterestedly over the near collision. In his youth, he'd been a reckless driver, and during the last five years, he had driven rarely, usually leaving that task to an employee. Silently, he reminded himself to be more careful; he wanted to reach the cabin without incident.

He'd left the hotel about six hours earlier at 2 a.m. The night before, Kevin had filled up the gas tank and put Brady's luggage in the car. In the back of the Jeep Kevin added a case of wine and a case of imported beer. Brady didn't ask for the booze, but Kevin couldn't imagine going to a remote cabin without it.

One of Kevin's purchases was a blond wig, similar in style and color to his own hair. Brady had used the adjoining door to enter Kevin's room. He slipped on the wig, a pair of sunglasses and the clothes Kevin had been wearing a few hours earlier. Exiting through Kevin's hotel room door, he hastily made his way to the parking garage, careful to avoid getting too close to anyone Kevin knew. If someone saw him from afar, the person would assume Brady was the assistant. Brady didn't stop to consider that someone might think it odd he was wearing sunglasses at two in the morning.

The wig and sunglasses had been removed when he was safely away from the hotel. He'd been on the desolate highway for several hours, passing just a few vehicles. According to the map, it was less than an hour to Shipley, and from there, another ten or fifteen minutes to the cabin. He had just pulled into Canyon City, and according to the map, it was the last town he'd be going through until reaching the mountain village.

Turning the ignition off, he slipped the sunglasses

back on and glanced up into the rearview mirror and noticed the Suburban was parked behind him, waiting for a turn at the pump. He didn't see the driver; she had obviously gotten out of the car.

Without giving her a second thought, Brady opened the car door and exited the vehicle. According to the sign on the pump, he needed to go into the gas station and pay the teller before he could pump the gas. Shutting the car door behind him, he turned abruptly and ran into the driver of the Suburban.

The two stood silently in the parking lot for a brief moment. Brady inwardly groaned, certain this woman would recognize him and start making a scene. He was in no mood for another adoring fan. He hoped the sunglasses would help conceal his identity.

Instead of the accolades he expected, the woman shot him a look of disgust and mumbled something under her breath before walking around him and making her way to the minimart section of the gas station.

Did she just call me an ass? Brady silently asked himself. He frowned and followed her into the building. They were the only two people in the station, save for the teller, who was an elderly man sitting on a stool behind the counter, reading a newspaper. The man glanced up briefly, and then went back to reading.

The woman didn't go immediately to the teller, but went to the self-serve refreshment section and poured herself a hot cup of coffee. *That's a good idea.* Brady thought. He could use some caffeine.

Instead of paying for his gas, he walked toward the woman. She glanced up and he again waited for her to recognize him. Had the station been full of people, he would have avoided her attention, but since they were virtually alone, he thought it would be amusing to watch her recognize him and witness her blush of embarrassment for calling him an ass. He imagined she'd be offering to pour his coffee while making up some lame excuse for her earlier comment.

Ella glanced up and watched the man from the Jeep approach. She wondered briefly, why he was practically smirking. It was obvious he wasn't contrite for cutting off the Suburban. He just stood there a moment, staring at her. She didn't know if he was trying to figure out what to say or was simply waiting for her to get out of his way. The notion occurred to Ella that he half expected her to hand him her cup of coffee. She told herself she should be grateful he wasn't shoving her out of his way or snatching the cup from her hand. Silently, Ella's gaze swept over the arrogant stranger and then she walked past him, without looking back or making a comment.

Brady frowned, then turned and watched her

walk to the counter. He couldn't help but notice the sexy little sway of her cute backside, as she walked away from him. Smiling, Brady was confident that if he wanted, he could remove her denims with minimal effort. He had to admit she was attractive, in a wholesome, country girl kind of way. He typically dated high maintenance women, who photographed well. It had been years since he'd taken a casual fan to his bed. It was too bad he didn't have the time, Brady told himself as he filled a Styrofoam cup with hot coffee.

"Morning, Ed," Brady heard the woman say to the man reading the newspaper. She set her coffee cup on the counter and reached into her purse for her wallet.

"Hey, Ella, I didn't realize that was you. With my reading glasses on, anything beyond a couple feet is a blur. Have you finished your next bestseller?" Removing his reading glasses, Ed stood up. Still holding the glasses in one hand, he folded the newspaper he had been reading and tossed it on the stool.

"I'm working on it. My editor says if I get the manuscript to her by the first of December it might actually be out before Christmas."

"I'll be sure to let Carol know. She wanted me to tell you she loved the last one, by the way."

"Glad to hear that, Ed. Tell her hi for me." She handed Ed two twenty dollar bills. "I need forty dollars' worth."

Ed gave her a little nod and wink, and then watched her walk toward the exit and out the door before turning to Brady, who was now standing at the counter.

"She's an author," Ed announced to Brady after Ella left the building.

"Oh?" Brady glanced from Ed to the front door. He could see Ella through the glass pane walking toward her vehicle. Brady looked back at Ed. It was obvious the old man had no idea who he was. That didn't particularly surprise Brady, considering the man's age.

"Yep, she's my wife's favorite author. I haven't read her books, mind you. She writes stuff women like to read, you know, romance. But we're pretty proud of our Ella. She's our local celebrity."

"I take it she's from around here," Brady asked, mildly curious.

"Sure is," Ed said proudly.

"What did you say her name is?" Brady asked, wondering if he had heard of her.

"Ella Lewis. But she writes under another name, and I never can remember it."

"Do you know who her publisher is?" Brady asked as he handed Ed money for the gas.

"Oh, she publishes her own stuff," Ed explained.

"Really?" Brady smiled and glanced toward the door. Not long ago he'd met with a publisher regarding his biography. The two got into a discussion over the recent trend of wannabe writers who jumped into self-publishing. *Lazy, no talent hacks,* the publisher termed the upstarts. The man went on to say most independent authors made very little from their efforts, and Brady suspected this Ella was probably lucky to sell a few books to her friends. He couldn't imagine she actually made a living writing romance novels without the assistance of an agent and real publisher.

Ella waited patiently for the man to return to the Jeep and get gas, so she could fill up the Suburban's tank. If the second pump wasn't out of order, she would have moved her car, but that pump had been out of order for over a week now.

She planned to stop at her favorite diner after getting gas to have breakfast before heading back to her condominium to pick up Sam. According to the morning weather report, a storm was moving in, but she intended to be at the cabin by noon, and she hoped to miss the bad weather. She wasn't overly concerned about reaching the cabin safely because her vehicle was a four-wheel drive, and she wasn't traveling in the dark.

Brady filled his tank and wondered briefly, why the woman simply didn't use the other gas pump. He didn't notice the out of order sign. When he finished, he got back into the Jeep and drove off without looking back.

According to the map, there wasn't much but

vacant highway from his current location to the village of Shipley. He should be there in less than an hour. Hungry, Brady decided to have a quick breakfast before getting back on the highway. Keeping his left hand on the steering wheel, he took a sip of his coffee, and then set the Styrofoam cup between his legs. He grabbed the blond wig from the passenger's seat and hastily fit it on his head.

ELLA NOTICED THE JEEP THE MOMENT SHE PULLED UP TO the diner. After parking the Suburban, she got out of her car, clicked the remote attached to her keychain to lock the vehicle, and walked to the diner's front door.

It was fairly busy, and the only empty booth was adjacent to a man with shaggy blond hair. She glanced around, didn't see the driver of the Jeep and suspected he was in the restroom. As she walked past the booth with the blond man, he turned and looked at her. He wore sunglasses. Her eyes widened slightly when she realized he was the man from the Jeep.

Without making a comment, she sat at an empty booth and hastily picked up the menu that was already on the table. Trying to hide behind the menu, she scooted down in her seat.

What is he, some kind of a nut? Ella asked herself,

certain he'd recognized her from the gas station. *What kind of a man wears a silly blond wig?* When she glanced up over the menu, toward his table, she noticed he was staring at her. He immediately looked down at his menu.

She suddenly remembered Amanda discussing the rock star who rented the cabin and how he wanted to keep his stay a secret. *Could that be him?* Ella asked herself. She tried to remember what Brady Gates looked like. When it came to remembering faces, she had poor facial recognition skills. Setting the menu on the table, Ella reached into her purse and pulled out her iPhone.

As she went online to do a quick search for Brady Gate images, a waitress walked up to her table. Without setting down the phone, Ella gave the waitress her order and continued with the online search.

A few seconds later Ella had her answer. The man in the next booth was Brady Gates. Ella wasn't excited to discover the famous rock star was just a few feet away, but she was relieved he wasn't some serial killer that might run her off the road while she drove down the highway, and cut her into little pieces.

Ella smiled, put her phone back in her purse, and added cream to the coffee the waitress had just brought her.

Brady felt like an idiot sitting in the booth wearing the damn wig. While the waitress didn't seem to recognize him with the dark glasses and blond hair, it was obvious the woman from the gas station recognized him from earlier. So far, it didn't seem as if she knew his real identity. If she did, he imagined she would at least be asking for his autograph by now.

Getting another look at the woman, he had to admit she was attractive. He was half-tempted to give her a tumble, yet considering she was some wannabe writer, he had no doubt she'd exploit their sexual encounter to get more readers. She might have a nice ass, and sexy eyes, but she wasn't worth the trouble.

Determined to get out of the diner before the woman came over and started pestering him, Brady wolfed down his breakfast and was heading out the door by the time the server brought Ella her food.

Ella chuckled to herself as she watched Brady throw money on the table and rush out the door to the Jeep. She looked out the window and watched him pull out of the parking lot. She could swear she saw him pull the silly blond wig from his head.

When Ella finished breakfast, she paid the server and headed back to her condominium to pick up Sam. She found her dog waiting patiently by the door, ready to leave. She gave her home a final inspection, making sure everything was turned off and windows and doors were all locked, which delayed her trip another fifteen minutes. She was surprised to find the sky much darker than it had been when she'd gone inside just minutes earlier.

Overhead heavy dark clouds replaced puffy white formations. No longer stationary, they drifted steadily as if someone was calling them together for some ominous purpose.

"Looks like that storm is coming, Sam," Ella said to her dog as she opened the back door of the vehicle. Sam jumped up and put her front paws along the floorboard behind the driver's seat. Ella reached down and picked up the dog's rear end, helping the canine get into the car. Ella gave Sam's rump an affectionate little pat before closing the door. Sam quickly moved onto the back seat and lay down.

CHAPTER FOUR

"Fuck," Brady cursed as snowflakes thinly coated the windshield. The wiper's steady back and forth proved ineffective at removing the persistent white downpour. With limited visibility, Brady struggled to keep his full attention on the uncertain road ahead.

The storm hit the moment he reached Shipley. Finding the hamlet was an easy enough task. All he had to do was stay on the correct highway and head in a specific direction. He was surprised it was such a tiny community. Located at the base of the mountain its business district was comprised of one street, flanked by a number of vintage log cabins long since converted for commercial use. The village appeared to have just one gas station and one restaurant. According to Kevin, it was typically a summer destination, and Brady wondered about the people who lived in the village fulltime. Apparently, Kevin's cousin was one such resident, but he did not intend to meet her.

Locating the cabin was proving more challenging than finding the village. The directions were comprised of a long series of turn right, left and right again on winding mountain roads. Brady pulled over to the side of the desolate street and stopped for a moment to take out the directions Kevin had given him. He opened the piece of paper, read it and then tossed it on the passenger seat.

Not only were the wipers having a difficult time clearing away the snow, the Jeep's heater was not keeping the cab warm. It had stopped producing hot air about fifteen minutes after leaving the diner. Grabbing a coat from the back seat, he slipped it on before starting back up the road.

The amount of snow falling increased substantially and appeared to be coming down faster and faster. Brady slowed the Jeep and leaned closer to the windshield, looking up the road through a thick curtain of snowfall. He squinted, having a difficult time seeing beyond the icy glass. The scraping sound of the wipers filled his ears, but beyond that, it seemed oddly silent. The radio had stopped working thirty minutes earlier, and he turned it off when the only sound coming from the speakers was static-laden music.

It had been about fifteen minutes since he'd

pulled out of the village, and so far, he hadn't seen another car. He passed several cabins along the way, yet they all seemed to be vacant. Shivering, he chewed his lower lip nervously, starting to feel a bit uneasy. The road was getting steeper, and already, snow covered the asphalt. The persistent snowfall hampered his vision, making it difficult to read the road signs.

He reached out and again fumbled with the heating controls. Placing his hand over the vent, he cursed and wondered why he couldn't feel warm air. Glancing at the speedometer and noting the mileage, he estimated he had passed the last cabin about a mile or more back. The road was getting steeper, and he knew his next turn was up ahead, perhaps after he reached the top of the incline.

The Jeep was having a problem getting up the icy road. Pressing his foot harder on the gas pedal, the engine made a revving noise, but instead of going forward, it stayed in place, its tires making a painful spinning sound. Brady cringed, realizing he hadn't put the vehicle in four-wheel drive.

The previous day, Kevin had given him instructions on how to put the Jeep in four-wheel drive, but Brady couldn't remember what to do. Had he not been so cold or didn't feel as if he was being smothered under a mountain of snow, he might have remembered. He felt the car slipping backwards down the hill, and panic set in. Frantically, he slammed his foot on the brake and then on the gas pedal.

His erratic gyrations actually got the Jeep moving up the hill again, and when he reached the top, where the road took a dip, he abruptly hit the gas petal, sending the Jeep wildly out of control. The tires hit a patch of black ice, and helplessly, Brady held tightly onto the steering wheel as the Jeep drove off the road into a snowy ditch, where it firmly planted itself.

After a few moments, he realized there was no way to get out of the ditch without four-wheel drive. Still unable to recall the instructions, he pulled out his cell phone to call Kevin. He felt foolish for having to ask, but he did not intend to spend the day stuck in the snow.

"Whose fucking idea was a trip to the mountains in the middle of a blizzard?" Brady grumbled as he turned off the ignition. The only other sound in the vehicle was that of the windshield wipers, still moving back and forth, while snow covered the Jeep.

"I don't believe this!" Brady groaned when he realized he could not get cell service. He closed his eyes and leaned his head back for a moment. With the ignition turned off, he found the sound of the wipers scraping back and forth more annoying than before. Opening his eyes, he leaned forward and looked at the dashboard, searching for some way to turn off the wipers. He found it. Instantly, he was immersed in eerie silence.

Brady took a deep breath and told himself to stay calm; after all, it was just a little snow. If he had to, he could walk back to the last cabin he'd seen and use their phone to call for a tow truck. It was only about a mile back, and he should be able to handle that easily, even with the storm.

He tried one more time to put the Jeep in four-wheel drive without success. He wondered if the cell phone might work down the road a bit. Perhaps he was just in a dead zone. The boots he was wearing were warm enough and comfortable to walk in, but they weren't waterproof. He hadn't intended to go trudging around in the snow, so he had not had Kevin purchase snow boots.

Reaching around to the back seat, he opened his suitcase and took out a sweatshirt. He removed his jacket, and slipped the sweatshirt on over his shirt. He then put his jacket back on, zipping up its front.

Since he didn't have any gloves, he grabbed a pair of dry socks for his hands and was tempted to slip a second pair on his feet, but was afraid that would make his shoes too tight and uncomfortable. He cursed himself for not bringing a warm cap, and then looked at the blond wig. Giving a shrug, he grabbed the wig and fit it on his head. Before opening the door, he slipped the cell phone in his jacket pocket.

Outside the Jeep, he was greeted with wet, slushy

snow instead of dry powder. Walking from the Jeep's position in the snow-filled ditch to the road proved more challenging than he expected. By the time he reached the snow-covered pavement, his pants were drenched from the knees down.

Determine to head back down the road in the direction from which he came, he discovered walking downhill and staying erect was nearly impossible. His right foot misstepped, sending him tumbling backwards onto the road. Sprawled helplessly on his backside, his arms extended outward, he looked like someone preparing to make a snow angel. With great effort, he managed to stand back up on his feet, yet now, not only was the lower portion of his pants legs wet, so was the fabric covering his buttock and the back of his jacket.

The fall had shifted the wig to an odd angle, but in his discomfort, he failed to notice and did not straighten the head covering. The socks on his hands were now soaking wet, so he removed them and tossed them to the road. Shivering, he buried his hands in his coat pockets and started down the road again, determined to stay on his feet.

His determination was not enough to keep him firmly upright, and he landed twice more on his backside before reaching the bottom of the incline. Along the way, he continually checked for cell phone reception, but found none.

Ella loved her Suburban. When she initially purchased the vehicle, her sister had teased her, asking why she wasn't driving something sportier, like a Mercedes Coupe or BMW. As she made her way up the snowy mountain, she was happy to be driving the sturdy four-wheel drive vehicle.

It was a beautiful day, and she appreciated the snow. The first thing she would do when she reached her cabin was build a fire and put on a pot of home-made chili. Ella glanced down at the clock. It was a quarter to noon. She smiled and settled down in the car seat, enjoying the way the snow fell across the windshield. Ella thought it looked magical.

Sam was no longer sleeping, but was now looking out the window, sensing they were close to their destination. They'd already passed several cabins, and she could tell they were all vacant.

Just as she wondered about the rock star and if he had made it to the cabin before the snowstorm, she saw him staggering down the snow-laden road with the strange blond wig sitting cockeyed on his head. He walked zombie-like in her direction, as if he was unaware of the oncoming vehicle.

"Holy crap!" Ella shouted, causing Sam to pick up her ears and let out a little bark. It was obvious his Jeep had broken down. Where it was, she had no clue, but by the looks of him, he had been walking for a while, and if she didn't get him warm and dry, he would catch pneumonia. Unfortunately, pneumonia was probably the least of his worries. Ella immediately thought of frostbite.

Ella sped up, pulled the Suburban alongside Brady, and put the vehicle in park. He stopped walking and looked at the car as if he was surprised at its sudden appearance. Ella leaned over the backseat, and opened the car door, ordering Brady inside the vehicle. She made a snap decision to put him in the back seat for the drive to her cabin. Sam would provide the foolish rock star necessary warmth.

Brady didn't hesitate. He climbed into the backseat, and closed the door behind him. If Brady was afraid of the Australian shepherd sharing the seat with him, or annoyed with the dog's persistent sniffing and nose nudging, it wasn't apparent by the way Brady immediately wrapped his arms around the furry dog, soaking up the canine's warmth. Sam seemed to understand, and patiently endured the stranger's manhandling.

Unable to tolerate the sight of the silly wig a moment longer, Ella snatched it from Brady's head and tossed it on the front passenger seat before putting the vehicle back in gear and starting up the road.

"The...Je..Je...Jeep...we need to get it," Brady stammered, as his body shivered uncontrollably.

"I assume it's at the side of the road someplace."

Ella's annoyance was obvious. Brady wondered why she sounded so angry, considering he was the one who was freezing while she was nice and dry.

"Yes, we… we need to get it."

"I don't think so. We're getting you to my cabin where you can get out of those clothes and dry off, before you get a nasty case of frostbite." *If you haven't already*, she added silently.

"No…no…" Brady shivered. "I've rented a cabin. Please take me there, I'll pay you."

"Sorry, but my cabin's closer. I'm taking you there," Ella said stubbornly.

"I'm not having sex with you," Brady insisted, still shivering uncontrollably as he tried to absorb the dog's warmth. This was his nightmare. He was going to be held captive by some deranged fan. It was obvious she'd followed him up to the mountain.

"Excuse me?" Ella shrieked. *Did I hear him right?*

"I'm just making it perfectly clear," Brady answered as he continued to hug Sam. "I appreciate that you picked me up, and I'll be happy to pay you for your services, but if you thought following me up here would…"

"You think I followed you up here?"

"Didn't you?" He was unable to stop shivering, making his voice raspy.

"Why, you jackass! I should have left you on the side of the road to freeze. No, I didn't follow you up here. And if I had, how would I have known you would be so reckless as to go wandering out in a blizzard?"

Brady considered her words for a moment, and realized she had a point.

"I'm sorry. I just assumed. Why… why are you up here?"

"I have a cabin up here. I believe I mentioned that a moment ago," Ella spat angrily. "Although, you do make such an attractive figure wearing that silly blond wig sideways," she added with a snort. At the mention of the wig, Brady felt his face flush. He suddenly realized how foolish he must have looked, stumbling down the road wearing the ill-fitting hairpiece.

It was obvious he pissed off his rescuer, so he decided to remain quiet for the rest of the drive. He needed to clear his head and reestablish feeling to his fingers and toes.

Minutes later, they pulled into the driveway of a large log cabin. Ella reached to the center console and pulled out the garage door opener. After giving it a click, the garage door began to open.

"When we get in the house, I'll start a hot shower for you, so you can get warm. Don't worry; your virtue is safe with me."

After driving into the garage and turning off the engine, Ella pushed the garage door opener again, sending the automatic door closing behind them. She quickly got from the vehicle. Glancing in the backseat, she saw Sam practically sitting on Brady's lap. Moving to the passenger side of the car, she opened the back door. Brady assumed she intended to help him out, so he immediately told her he could get out on his own. Ella glared at him and then asked him to please get out of the car so she could help her dog.

He wasn't sure why the dog needed help, but he got from the vehicle and stood shivering in the garage as Ella reached in the back seat and physically guided Sam down onto the concrete floor of the garage.

"Why doesn't she just jump out?" Brady asked, hugging his own body and still shivering.

"Because she can't," Ella said as she shot him another angry look. Without saying a word, she walked into the cabin, leaving Sam and Brady to follow in her wake.

CHAPTER FIVE

Ella went immediately to the downstairs bathroom and turned on the small wall heater. Silently, Brady, who was still trembling, followed her into the room with Sam trailing behind him. The dog stood in the doorway and watched as Brady started rubbing his hands together in front of the hot red coils of the space heater.

"You might have frostbite; I don't think you are supposed to rub your hands together like that. Get your wet clothes off and stick your hands under your armpits while I get the water warm," Ella instructed as she opened the shower door and turned on the hot water. She knew the water was icy cold, and would take a few minutes to warm up.

The two stood in the small space with Sam looking on. The dog sniffed the air around the wet stranger. Brady didn't seem embarrassed about stripping in front of Ella, and immediately jerked off his jacket, and then sweatshirt.

"I'm going to the kitchen and grab a thermometer. We don't want the shower to get over 110. Or was it 107? I'll be right back." As she walked around the now half-nude rock star, she nudged Sam out of the bathroom, into the hallway, and closed the door to keep the heat in the small room.

When she returned to the bathroom a few minutes later, she found Brady in the shower, standing under the hot water. The shower door was shut, yet through the obscure glass she could see the outline of his body. Ella paused for a moment, and felt a pang of embarrassment. She took a deep breath and told herself to grow up; this was a special circumstance. While she wasn't accustomed to being alone with strange nude men, she was fairly confident that she would be safe with this one.

"I'm going to open the shower door just a crack and hand you a thermometer. I know the hot water feels good, but you don't want the temperature to get over 107."

She opened the shower door an inch, and looked away as she handed him the thermometer. He took it from her and asked, "You aren't coming in?" There was a teasing lilt to his voice.

"Excuse me?" Ella slammed the shower door shut.

"Body heat and all," he laughed, feeling suddenly

much better. The sensation was back in his hands and feet, and by the look of his skin, he didn't imagine he had frostbite.

"Apparently, you are feeling better. You made it very clear I could not have my way with you," Ella said sarcastically.

"Now that I know you aren't Annie Wilkes, I'm okay with it."

"Well, gee, lucky me. Thanks, but no thanks. Stay in the shower while I bring you some dry towels and a blanket to wrap up in until your clothes dry." Ella reached down and picked his discarded clothing off the floor. "I'm going to go put these in the washing machine after I get you the towels and blanket." Ella left the bathroom, closing the door behind her before Brady could respond.

Brady stood under the hot water as it streamed from the showerhead. Enjoying the heat, he glanced down at the thermometer. The idea of testing the water temperature seemed silly, so he set the thermometer on the shelf in the shower, and closed his eyes, moving completely under the downpour.

A few minutes later, he heard the bathroom door open, and he could see the woman's silhouette through the obscuring glass. The toilet seat was down, and he watched as she set something on it, which looked like a stack of towels.

"I'm hanging the blanket on the back of the door,

so it doesn't get wet when you dry off," he heard her say before she left the room.

Ella went to the laundry room, adjacent to the doorway leading to the garage. Before putting the clothes in the washing machine, she checked all the pockets. The only thing she found was a wallet in his pants pocket, which she set on a shelf. She checked the label on the jacket, and it appeared to be washable, so she shoved the coat in the washing machine with his denims, shirt, sweatshirt and underwear. Turning off the laundry room light, she grabbed his wallet from the shelf and walked to the cabin's main downstairs living area, at the end of the hallway, just past the door to the bathroom where she'd left Brady.

Five years earlier, Ella's father remodeled the downstairs living area, removing the wall separating the small kitchen from the living room. Now, it was one great room with a breakfast bar separating the living room from the compact kitchen. When standing in the kitchen, she could look across the living room to the stone fireplace and the large picture window along the far wall.

After setting the wallet on the kitchen counter, she decided to call Amanda about the stranded renter. She didn't bother using her cell phone, as she already knew there was no cell service on the mountain. Picking up the landline, Ella let out a little curse when she realized the line was dead.

Glancing up from the phone, Ella looked out the

kitchen window and noticed the snow was coming down even harder than before. Setting the phone's handset back on its cradle, she walked into the living room to the large picture window behind the leather couch and opened the blinds so she could see outside.

"Damn, we're snowed in," Ella cursed as she stood at the window, looking out. Snow covered the landscape, making it impossible to distinguish where her front yard ended and the street began. A steady stream of snowflakes continued to fall from the sky.

"Snowed in?" Ella heard a voice ask behind her.

She turned around and faced her houseguest, who stood in the living room, a red, white and blue patchwork quilt wrapped around his nude body. His dark hair was damp and had obviously been towel dried and combed back hastily with his fingers. It fell to just above his shoulders.

Ella paused a moment, staring at him, before responding. He really did have amazing eyes. She could understand why star-struck women might be attracted to such a man.

"I'm afraid so. My name is Ella Lewis, by the way. I assume you're Brady Gates. Amanda told me you were renting a cabin up here."

"Amanda?" he asked with a frown.

"Yes, the woman who handles the rentals on the mountain."

"She wasn't supposed to tell anyone." He didn't

know why he should expect anything else. He imagined paparazzi would be showing up within the hour, if they weren't already here.

"Yeah, I heard that. But she just told me, 'cause she knew I'm safe to tell. Don't worry, she didn't tell anyone else."

"Why should I believe you wouldn't tell someone?" The moment Brady asked the question he came up with his own answer. *She wants to keep me to herself.*

"Well, for one reason, until she told me you were coming up here, I had no clue who you were. Now, if you'll excuse me." Dismissively, Ella walked from the living room to the hallway leading to the garage. "I'm going to bring in my stuff from the car. I need to get the food put away."

"What do you mean you had no clue who I was?" Brady called after her. He continued to stand in the center of the living room wrapped in the colorful blanket.

"Just what I said," Ella shouted back, not taking the time to explain.

When Ella disappeared down the hallway, Brady noticed his wallet sitting on the kitchen counter. He looked around but didn't see his cell phone. There was a telephone sitting on the counter. The cabin had a landline. He picked up the phone to call out but the line was dead.

"Do you have my cell phone?" Brady asked when

Ella walked back into the kitchen carrying a cardboard box filled with groceries.

"Excuse me? Why would I have your cell phone?"

"It was in my coat pocket."

"I checked your pockets before I put your clothes in the washing machine. The only thing I found was your wallet." She nodded to the wallet sitting on the counter.

"It must have fallen out in the back seat of your car."

"I didn't see it. But I'll look again when I go out there. Unfortunately, it won't do you any good," Ella said as she set the box on the kitchen counter.

"What do you mean?"

"No cell service up here." She turned and walked from the kitchen and headed back toward the garage.

"I don't believe you," Brady told her when she returned to the kitchen carrying her purse and a bag of groceries.

"What do you mean?" While bringing in the groceries a few moments earlier, she had thought to herself how ungrateful the man seemed, considering she'd just saved him from freezing to death on the mountain.

"I can't believe there's no cell service," he said. She glanced at him as she set her purse and the sack on the counter, and thought he looked rather silly with the quilt wrapped around him.

"See for yourself," Ella said impatiently as she

opened her purse, pulled out her iPhone and tossed it to Brady. "Yours wasn't in the car, but you can try mine."

Surprised by her sudden action, he awkwardly reached for the unexpected missal coming toward him, temporarily releasing his hold on the quilt. He fumbled for a moment and the covering dropped to his feet, giving Ella just a brief glimpse of what the groupies were desperate to see, before Brady quickly recovered himself.

Ella chuckled, finding the peep show more amusing than titillating, and turned away, heading back to the car.

Brady walked to the couch, sat down, and tried to make a phone call. Just as Ella said, it did not work. Frustrated at being stranded, Brady sat quietly and contemplated his situation while Ella brought in the rest of the groceries and her luggage. Sam kept close to Ella's side, following her in and out of the garage.

"Thanks for the help," Ella said sarcastically when she entered the kitchen and started to put the groceries away.

"This phone doesn't work." He got up from the couch and walked to the kitchen, then set her iPhone on the counter.

"Duh. Didn't I say that? I put your clothes in the dryer. They should be ready in a few minutes. Since you no longer look as if you might die of frostbite, I think you can manage to get them yourself when they're done."

"If the phone doesn't work, I need you to take me back to the Jeep so I can get my things, and then take me to the cabin I rented, or maybe back to town would be better."

"I don't think so," Ella said as she put a gallon of milk in the refrigerator.

"You can't keep me here," Brady insisted.

"Keep you here? What's with you?" Ella said angrily as she turned and faced her unwelcome houseguest. "You haven't so much as said *thank you.* If I hadn't stopped and dragged your butt out of the snow, you would probably be a Popsicle by now. You act like it's my fault the phone line is down, or that we don't have cell service. Sorry, buddy, but none of that is about me, or even you. It's just the simple reality of this place.

"If you think I intend to risk my life and go out in this weather, you're nuts. This is not driving weather. Unless you haven't noticed, we're having a fricking blizzard! You think I want you here? Trust me, if I could simply drive you someplace and drop you off, I would do that in a heartbeat."

"You sound like you mean that," Brady said in a quiet voice. Her angry tirade startled him. He assumed she was just making excuses to keep him at the cabin. She wouldn't be the first woman who tried to insinuate herself in his life, especially since she was given this opportunity. Yet, by her cross expression and the fact she rarely looked at him, he was beginning to suspect she genuinely did not like him.

"Do you dislike me?" Brady found himself asking when Ella went back to organizing her groceries. Ella paused and turned from the open pantry to face Brady.

"Dislike you? I don't even know you."

"Most people assume they know me. I just wondered if you read something about me that made you dislike me."

"Mr. Gates," Ella began after taking a deep breath, "I understand you are some sort of celebrity. The only reason I know that is because Amanda told me she rented the cabin to some well-known musician. I don't want to hurt your feelings, but frankly, when she told me your name, I had no clue who you were."

Brady found himself laughing at her words. He didn't know what he found more amusing, the fact that she pretended to have no idea who he was, or that she might hurt his feelings. He thought whatever game she was playing was mildly amusing, and had she not saved his life, he might be more annoyed.

"Miss….what did you say your name was again?" he asked in a condescending tone.

"Ella Lewis."

"Miss Lewis, I might believe what you're saying if I thought you'd been living on this mountain for the last five years, but considering you are supposedly a writer…"

"Supposedly?" Ella interrupted. "First of all, how did you know I was a writer? And what do you mean, supposedly?"

"The guy at the gas station mentioned it."

"Oh, you mean when you cut me off, and stole my place in line?"

"I didn't mean to do that."

"And I don't recall you apologizing. But then, you haven't yet thanked me for saving you from the blizzard, so I suppose manners are something you don't need when you obtain whatever fame you *supposedly* have. And you must have a hell of a lot of money, because if you're as popular with the women as Amanda claims, it certainly can't be your charm that reels them in." At that moment, the dryer bell rang.

"That's the dryer. Your clothes should be ready. Go get dressed. You look ridiculous in that quilt." Ella turned from Brady to put away the last bag of groceries.

Brady stood a moment in silence and watched Ella. She was definitely pissed, he told himself. If she was trying to play hard to get, she was a pretty good actress. Brady started down the hall and paused briefly at the bathroom he'd used earlier. Suddenly he recalled asking Ella to join him in the shower. He cringed at his behavior, not really sure why the crude invitation popped out of his mouth. He remembered feeling a sense of euphoria, knowing he was safe and warm, and suspected that was the reason for the spontaneous invite.

In the laundry room, Brady found his clothes in the drier. The jacket was still a bit damp, but the rest of the clothing was dry. Shutting the laundry room door for privacy, Brady slipped on the clothes he had been wearing earlier. They were actually Kevin's clothes, and he wished he had his suitcase with him so he could wear something he felt more comfortable in.

He tossed the damp jacket back in the dryer and turned on the machine. The quilt was on the floor, so he picked it up and folded it hastily, before setting it atop the washing machine.

On the way back to the living room and kitchen area, Brady stopped to use the bathroom. He found his boots still sitting on the floor, and picked them up after he finished washing his hands. The shoes were wet. He took them with him, looking for a warm place to put them so they could dry.

CHAPTER SIX

*B*rady found Ella in the living room, placing firewood in the stone fireplace. Her back was to him, and once again, Brady noticed her shapely backside, which looked especially appealing as she bent over the stone hearth to arrange the firewood. He had the sudden urge to step behind her, and grab her hips with his hands and pull her denim-clad bottom to his groin. Just the thought made him hard, but his hands held the wet boots and he had a feeling if he acted on his impulse she'd hit him over the head with a stick of firewood.

Brady couldn't recall the last time he'd experienced such an unexpected surge of lust. He wondered briefly if the heightened awareness of his own mortality during the snowstorm had flipped some primal switch. Perhaps the attraction was encouraged by her game of disinterest. He wasn't certain it wasn't an act. She wouldn't be the first woman who used scheming tactics to get his attention. The unbelievable part of her story was in trying to convince him she hadn't known who he was a few days earlier.

Ella was unaware of Brady's presence behind her, and the fact he stood quietly, studying her with carnal interest. After arranging the firewood and kindling, it didn't take her long to start the fire. Satisfied it would soon be blazing; she stood up and turned around, away from the stone fireplace.

Startled, Ella jumped slightly before letting out a little gasp and muttering a curse. "You frightened me!" she said angrily, then stomped around Brady into the kitchen area.

"I'm sorry. I was just watching you make the fire. Where can I put these to dry out?" He held up his boots to show her.

"You can put them on the hearth." Ella sounded annoyed.

Brady turned back to the fireplace and set the boots on the stone hearth before turning around again and walking toward the kitchen. Silently, he took a seat at the breakfast bar, and watched as Ella began taking groceries from the refrigerator.

"I do want to thank you for saving me. I'm sorry if I sounded ungrateful earlier, but I'll confess the mishap had me more upset than I realized." Brady watched as she removed butcher paper from what appeared to be a pound of ground beef.

Ella glanced up from what she was doing and met his gaze. *He is a handsome devil,* she told herself. Even if he wasn't some rock star, she imagined he could easily lure women to his bed with those blue eyes alone. The image of him stumbling through the snowstorm, the blond wig askew, partially covering his dark hair, popped in her head. She found herself smiling. He really had looked vulnerable and ridiculous when she found him, and she imagined he had been terrified.

"That's okay. I understand. Are you hungry? Do you like chili?" she asked cheerfully, no longer sounding annoyed.

"Actually, I'm hungry. Didn't realize it until you mentioned it. And yes, I like chili."

She gave him a soft smile and continued preparing the meal.

Brady watched her quietly for a few minutes. "How long do you think we'll be stuck here?" he finally asked, looking past her to the kitchen window. The snow still fell in heavy sheets.

"It just depends when the snow stops. It's still coming down hard. It's possible it'll stop sometime today, and if the snowplow makes it up here in the morning, the roads could be open by tomorrow afternoon. Unfortunately, we don't have television up here, and no radio reception so there is no way of finding out the current weather report. The last I heard, we were to get snow sometime today, and it was expected to last the rest of the week."

"Are you saying I could be stuck here for over a week?" Brady said incredulously.

"Actually, we could be stuck here for over a week even if the snow stops sometime today. I was trying to be optimistic, but they aren't especially prompt at clearing these roads. Nobody lives up here fulltime, and according to Amanda, she wasn't expecting anyone but you and me to come up here this weekend. Considering that we were planning to stay several weeks, and she knows we have supplies, I doubt we'll be top priority for the snowplow. If there's snow along the lower region, where the full-timers live, they'll get to those areas first. Just be grateful I didn't eat before I went grocery shopping," Ella told him as she began frying up the ground beef. "At least we won't starve."

"I don't understand." Brady frowned, having no idea what she was talking about.

"Well, you know what they say, never go grocery shopping on an empty stomach." She glanced at him, and then sighed at his clueless expression. "I guess you don't know. I suppose you have minions to do your shopping and other menial tasks."

"I have a staff. I don't know about minions," Brady replied, feeling suddenly awkward, which was not a familiar or comfortable sensation for him.

"Well, the rule of grocery shopping is to eat a meal first, or you end up buying more than what's necessary. Fortunately for you, I over-shopped at the market due to hunger pangs, and we should have enough food without severe rationing, even if this blizzard lasts longer than a few days. Of course, if we run out of food, you'll need to go hunting and bring us back a deer. You do know how to clean a deer don't you?" Ella asked her question with such calm seriousness that it proved impossible to contain her mirth when Brady responded with an expression of pure horror. It was obvious he thought she was serious.

"Hmm, I guess not," she said with a chuckle.

"Funny," Brady said dryly, feeling foolish. "So tell me, does that phone normally work?" He nodded toward the landline sitting on the kitchen counter.

"Yes, but apparently the lines are down. And I want to get this chili made before the electricity goes out. Times like this I regret we don't have natural gas up here, or at least a propane tank."

"You aren't serious?" Brady asked, certain she must have been teasing him as she had before about hunting.

"I'm afraid I am," Ella shrugged. She continued to

prepare the chili, which involved opening several cans of beans, whole tomatoes and chopping up fresh vegetables. "That's one reason I wanted to get the fire going. I already cranked up the heater, to get this place as warm as possible, just in case we do lose power. Before it gets dark outside, I'll get the flashlights, just in case."

"Is the cabin I rented really that far from here?" Brady asked.

"A mile or more. I've hiked up there before, but not in this weather."

"So you didn't find my cell phone in your car?"

"No, and I went through the back seat. Did you leave it in the Jeep?"

"I had it with me when I left the car. I was trying to find reception."

"This entire mountain is dead for cell service."

"Damn, I must have dropped it in the snow."

"Well, at least you don't have to worry about someone finding it and running up your phone charges," Ella said brightly. She covered the pan of chili, letting it simmer and then turned to face Brady. The counter separated them. "All we can do is make the best of a bad situation until this weather clears, or until the phone starts working again. I really make it a practice not to drive in this weather. Driving to the rental cabin is not as big as an issue for me as driving back here."

"I don't understand," Brady asked.

"Even with my four wheel-drive, going down the mountain when it's like this is pretty dangerous. To be honest, it kind of scares the crap outa me, driving down a steep hill when it's so icy. Maybe if I had chains, which I don't. Driving up hill is a little easier for me, and while it might be possible to get you to the rental cabin, I'm a little concerned about getting back here. And I really don't want to be stranded out on a snowy road, when no one knows I'm missing."

"I wouldn't want that." He hadn't considered he was asking her to risk her life by taking him to the rental cabin.

"It's just safer to stay here, until the storm breaks. You can sleep in one of the guestrooms."

"I just wish I had my suitcase," Brady muttered.

"How far from here is the Jeep?" Ella asked.

"Honestly, I'm not sure. I got a little disoriented after I slid off the road."

"Can you describe the area?"

Brady considered her question a moment before answering.

"I passed about a half dozen cabins, and the road was a steady incline. But then I came to an area where the road became much steeper. It was there I started having difficulty, and since I wasn't in four-wheel drive, I'm not sure how, but I made it to the top. Unfortunately, when the road started to level off a bit, I went off the side of the road, barely missing two pine trees. Now that I think about it, those two trees looked different than most of the other trees along the road, they..."

"Looked as if they had been in a fire?" Ella finished for him.

"Yes, they did."

"And the Jeep's near that spot?"

"Yes, it is. In a ditch, just a short distance from those trees."

"Actually, that really isn't far from here, if you cut through the forest, behind my cabin. Sam and I often take walks through that area."

"Your boyfriend?" Brady asked, feeling inexplicably disappointed to think she had a boyfriend.

At the mention of her name, Sam got up from where she was laying by the fireplace, and walked into the kitchen, wagging her short tail.

"Yes, girl, we're talking about you," Ella said as she patted Sam's back and leaned down to kiss the top of the dog's head before standing up again. "No, my dog."

"Sam. You named *her* Sam?" Brady asked. The dog walked from the kitchen to Brady and stuck her nose in his crotch. Gently, he moved her nose while stroking her furry neck. He hadn't forgotten how she provided warmth when he so needed it.

"Technically, it's Samantha. But dog names really shouldn't be three syllables."

"Is she a border collie?" he asked, still stroking Sam's furry backside.

"No, Australian shepherd. But her coloring is similar to a border collie. When I was younger, my parents had an Aussie, and her coloring was much more patchy. I don't recall anyone ever asking if she was a border collie, but I get that a lot with Sam. The border collies I've seen are normally black and white, whereas Sam also has brown markings. Plus, they tend to dock the Aussies' tails, whereas they don't the border collie."

"Why can't she get out of the Suburban on her own?" Brady asked.

"She was the runt of the litter, and I suspect that might be the cause of her medical issues. If you watch how she runs, it's as if she's double jointed. Her front legs remind me of how a swimmer doggy paddles. According to the vet, she has a very mild form of hip dysplasia. Sometimes she just falls down when she walks. On these hardwood floors, she does that more frequently. Sometimes she'll jump out of the car on her own, but normally, she's very apprehensive about leaping down without help. And she can't get in without a boost. She's my special needs dog."

"Where did you get her?" Brady asked.

"I bought her from a local woman who raises Aussies."

"Why didn't you ask for your money back?" Brady asked.

"Excuse me?"

"I assume when you purchase a dog from a breeder they come with some sort of a guarantee."

"Yes, but that would mean I'd have to give her back."

"But couldn't you get another, healthy dog?"

"Are you serious?"

Brady glanced up from Sam and looked at Ella. By the expression on her face, it was obvious he had offended the woman. He found her look of distain quite disconcerting.

"I'm sorry; I was just asking a question. I didn't mean to offend you," Brady said, still somewhat confused.

"Have you ever had a dog?" Ella asked.

"No."

"Are you serious?" Ella found it incomprehensible that he had never had a dog.

"No. I'm afraid pets weren't an option when I was growing up. Just another mouth to feed." It was no secret that Brady Gates came from poverty. Of course, that was not something Ella would know.

"Well, Sam's not just a dog," Ella explained, "She's family. She can't be replaced like a defected piece of furniture."

"I did appreciate her warmth." Brady smiled at the dog, who seemed quite content to rest her chin on his knee.

"She's a great dog," Ella said proudly, noticing that Sam did seem fond of the stranger.

"I never had much experience with dogs. Kevin tried to talk me into getting one a while back. More for security. He was talking rott or pit."

"Who is Kevin?" Ella asked as she turned to check on the pot of chili simmering on the stove.

"He's my assistant-slash-bodyguard."

"Oh, that's right. I think that's Amanda's cousin. You really need a bodyguard?" The way she asked the question Brady knew it was a serious inquiry.

"You really had no clue about who I was, did you?" Brady asked the question, no longer confident she was playing some coy game.

"I'm sorry," Ella apologized. "Please don't take it personal. It's not you. But I really don't watch that much television, and I've never been one to read fan or gossip magazines."

"Even those tabloids at the grocery store checkout stand?" Brady chuckled.

In reply, Ella wrinkled her nose and shook her head. She stood over the stove stirring the chili. "Especially those tabloids!" she said at last, after putting the lid back on the pan.

"And you don't like music?"

"Sure, I like music. I just never remember the names of the bands."

"So, you might be familiar with my music, and you just don't know it's mine?" Brady asked, wondering if she would start acting like another fawning fan once she realized what songs were his.

"Well, actually," Ella began as she pulled a block of cheddar cheese from the refrigerator and a grater from the cabinet, "when Amanda told me who was renting the cabin, and I didn't recognize your name, she tried singing one of your songs."

"And?" Brady asked, waiting for some response.

"Yeah, I recognized it." She grated the cheese onto a plate, refusing to look up from her task. She was embarrassed to admit she didn't like his music.

"So, you do know who I am?" Brady asked.

"Well, I guess, in a way. I Googled you when I got home, to see if I recognized your face. Do you always wear that makeup when you're in concert?" She asked the question about the makeup as if she thought it looked foolish.

"You looked at my Wikipedia page. Yes, it's my trademark."

"Oh." Ella dismissed the topic and took two bowls from the cabinet. "Are you ready for some chili?" she asked brightly.

"You don't like my music, do you?" Brady asked, sounding somewhat appalled at the idea. While he suspected some of the women who chased him might be more turned on by his fame and fortune than his music, he wasn't prepared for Ella's utter indifference.

"Hey, it's not you, really. I just sorta prefer country and soft rock." Ella smiled weakly, looking profoundly apologetic. Brady wasn't sure how to respond; he was in unchartered territory.

Instead of asking more questions, he accepted a bowl of chili topped with cheddar cheese, and a glass of iced cold milk. He ate the meal in silence, as he contemplated his current predicament.

CHAPTER SEVEN

"What, exactly, do you need from your Jeep?" Ella asked as she cleared away the dirty dishes.

Brady stood, intending to help her clean up after the meal, but she told him to sit down, that it would only take her a minute. Plus, there wasn't much room in the tiny kitchen area. He sat back down on the bar stool and watched her gather up the dishes and put the leftovers away.

"I'm not sure what you mean," he told her.

"Well, if we're able to make it to the Jeep, exactly what would you want to bring back? I've no idea how much you packed, and if we haul the stuff in this weather, through the snow, I'd rather just get the necessities."

"You think that'll be possible, to get my things from the Jeep?" Brady asked, hopeful.

"Yes, if it stops snowing; we could go in the morning. I've some snowshoes stored in the attic, and a sled we could pull to carry your stuff. It's really not that far, and we should be able to make it wearing the snowshoes, fairly easily."

"That'd be great. Everything I need is in one suitcase: my clothes, iPad. I'd love to get my phone, but I don't imagine I'll have much luck finding that. Getting the iPad would enable me to get some work done."

"Well, we don't have Internet here. I had it turned off at the end of the season."

"Why did you do that? Not that I need Internet for my work."

"The only reason the cabin has Internet service and cable during the summer, is because Amanda says renters expect it. I prefer not to have it; it's too much a distraction. When I come up here to write, I need to write, not surf and visit with my Facebook friends. Too much of a time killer. So, what kind of work does a rock star do on an iPad?" Ella asked, as she placed the leftover chili in the refrigerator.

"Must you refer to me as a *rock star*?" It wasn't the term that bothered him but how she said it, as if she was trying to humor him and found the notion of rock-stardom less than impressive.

"I'm sorry. Then, what do you tell people you do, when someone asks?" Ella's question was sincere, albeit a bit naive. When people asked her what she did for a living, she was never quite sure how to answer. Should she refer to herself as an author, or a writer? Both answers triggered more questions, and people often responded as if they didn't quite believe her, or would ask the name of her publisher. Since she published her own books, some of the responses were unkind.

"When people ask? No one asks me that." He wondered if she was serious.

Ella looked at him for a moment before she understood his confusion over her simple question. "You mean because everyone knows you? Oh, come on, you can't tell me everyone you meet already knows who you are." By his expression, she could tell that was exactly what he meant.

"You knew who I was," Brady reminded her.

"But that's only because Amanda told me. If she hadn't, what would you be telling me now, about what you do for a living?"

"You would've still picked me up, not knowing who I am?"

"Well, certainly. I couldn't very well let you freeze to death. So, what would you have said?" Ella was getting curious.

"I would have told you my name," Brady explained.

"And?" Ella prodded, waiting for his complete answer.

"And what? Once I told you my name, you'd know what I did."

Ella began to laugh.

"What's so funny?" He asked with a scowl.

"I told you, Amanda explained who you were. If she hadn't, your name—as well as your face—would mean nothing to me."

"What about my music? You told me you knew my music," he said, sounding somewhat insulted.

"So, when you meet someone who doesn't know you, you break into song when they ask what you do for a living." Ella began to giggle uncontrollably at the notion.

Brady sat quietly at the breakfast bar and watched with annoyance as the attractive young woman laughed heartily at his expense. "Of course not," he snapped.

"Oh, don't get all sensitive on me," Ella said once she had her giggles under control. "But you have to admit, the notion of you breaking into song when someone asks what you do for a living is pretty funny. Then let me ask you something else. What kind of work do you do on an iPad?"

"I'm working on some new songs. That's why I came up here, to get away by myself. I just wanted to work without any distractions."

"I can definitely relate. That's why I'm here. At home, there is always someone calling me on the phone, and I'm continually wandering off on the Internet, or I find myself chatting on Facebook. Before I know it, the day is gone and I've only written a couple hundred words. I don't see any reason we can't both accomplish what we came here for, in spite of the storm. I've plenty of food, and when the roads are clear, I can take you to your cabin. The only thing—we'll need to work in separate rooms."

"Separate rooms?" Brady asked. Although he couldn't imagine working on his music while she was in the same room moving around, it surprised him that she felt the same way as he did. He couldn't recall the last time a woman he met didn't use whatever means possible to keep close by his side when given the opportunity.

"I can't write when anyone else is in the room. I can't even have music playing. Music…oh, I imagine writing music involves making noise?"

"My iPad has a piano keyboard I use." He was amused that she referred to his music as noise. She seemed sincerely concerned with the possibility he might be too close in proximity to her while they worked.

"I sometimes use the spare room upstairs as an office. I guess I could do that," she suggested.

"I also, have headphones," Brady told her.

"Well, I'm sure we'll work something out. Now, if

you'll excuse me, I need to get supplies together, in case the electricity goes out."

"What can I help you with?" Brady asked as he got up from the bar stool and glanced out the living room window. The snow was still falling, and from his perspective, it looked to be fairly deep.

"This cabin has three bedrooms," Ella began. "Two upstairs and one downstairs. I'll be using the one I normally use, upstairs, and I thought you could use the one downstairs. There are clean sheets in the laundry room. Why don't you go ahead and put sheets on your bed, while I gather up supplies. When we're done, maybe I can get you to go up in the attic with me, before the sun sets, to get the snowshoes. It's kinda creepy up there, and I wouldn't mind the company."

"Certainly."

Ella flashed him a smile and started up the staircase, which was just off the living room and adjacent to the hallway. As she reached the second step, she stopped and turned to face her houseguest.

"Brady," she began.

He realized it was the first time she had called him by his name.

"I'm glad you're a famous rock star." Ella sounded relieved.

"Why is that?"

"Well...." She paused a moment before continuing, trying to find the right words. "Since you're a rock star, I know I'd be the last person who'd interest you sexually; therefore I don't have to worry about sleeping with a baseball bat." Ella smiled brightly, as if she was quite pleased with how she had worked things out in her head.

Brady didn't know how to respond to such a statement, so he said nothing. Apparently, she'd forgotten about his crude invitation to join him in the shower. She flashed him another quick smile, and then made her way up the stairs, leaving him alone on the first floor, watching her ascent.

On the second floor, Ella found what she was looking for—a box she'd placed in the linen closet during her last visit to the cabin. She removed it from the shelf and set it on the floor before opening its lid. In the cardboard container were six new flashlights that she'd picked up at Costco several months earlier. She tested each one to see if the batteries she'd installed were still in working order.

In the past, she'd kept just one flashlight at the cabin. After Amanda informed her it was missing, she went to Costco to pick up a new one, and ended up buying six instead of one. After checking the batteries, she took three of the flashlights with her and walked down the hallway.

The first stop was the bedroom she sometimes used as an office when at the cabin. On one wall was a set of bunk beds, and next to it was a nightstand.

Across from the bunk beds, under the window, was a large oak desk. She set one of the flashlights on the desk. The next stop was the upstairs guest bathroom. She put a flashlight in a bathroom drawer, next to the sink. She left the third flashlight in the master bedroom.

Ella returned to the box, picked it up and headed back to the first floor. She found Brady in the downstairs bedroom. He'd already put a set of sheets on the mattress and was just throwing a down comforter over the top sheet when Ella walked into the room.

"Here," she said, handing him a flashlight.

Brady took it and glanced down at it briefly, and then up at Ella.

"Go ahead and keep it next to your bed," she explained. "I'll be putting one in the downstairs bathroom, and another on the kitchen counter, in case the electricity goes out."

"Thanks," Brady said with a smile. He set the flashlight on the nightstand and watched Ella leave the room.

When he finished making the bed, he stepped out in the hall and noticed Ella picking up some luggage she had set there earlier.

"Can I help?" Brady asked.

"Sure, if you don't mind, you could bring those upstairs." She nodded to two cases still sitting on the floor. One held her laptop, the other the manual typewriter.

Brady quickly snatched up the two cases and followed Ella upstairs to the master bedroom. On his way up the stairs, he glanced toward the living room and noticed Sam sleeping soundly by the fireplace.

While walking down the upstairs hallway, he looked in the doorway of the first bedroom and noticed the bunk beds. He was relieved Ella put him downstairs, in a queen sized bed. When they reached her bedroom, his immediate thought was, *I want this room.*

It was a master suite with an adjoining bathroom. Its bed was much larger than his downstairs, and sported an antique brass headboard and vintage red and white quilt.

At least six plump pillows, each encased in its own white linen pillowcase, were stacked neatly along the head of the mattress, resting against the headboard in an inviting pile. What especially attracted his attention was the oversized picture window on the opposite wall.

Before he had a chance to comment on the room, Ella turned around, set the luggage on the floor, pointed out the door, and said, "Oh, those go in the bedroom down the hall."

Brady gave her a smile, then turned and headed back down the hallway toward the room with the bunk beds. He had every intention of returning to her room after depositing the cases in the other bedroom. Brady wanted a look out the large picture window that appeared to have a spectacular view of the area surrounding the cabin. Yet, he had taken only a few steps down the hallway when he heard the door to the master bedroom shut and a clicking sound. She had locked the door.

CHAPTER EIGHT

*A*fter setting the two cases in the spare bedroom, Brady walked back into the hallway and found Ella coming out of her bedroom, shutting the door behind her.

"I was going to take a shower and change my clothes when I remembered we need to go up into the attic and get the snowshoes and sled," Ella explained.

"Do you still want me to go with you?"

"If you don't mind. That place kinda creeps me out." Ella walked toward Brady, who stood in the middle of the hallway.

"You're afraid of your attic?" he teasingly inquired.

"Chalk it up to a childhood phobia brought on by an overactive imagination and a scary story my older cousin loved to tell me."

"Sounds interesting; I'm listening." His tone was friendlier and more relaxed than it had been after she first rescued him. *He has a nice smile,* Ella thought, noticing his straight white teeth. Pausing a moment, her gaze drifted from his mouth to his vivid blue eyes and she was startled by their striking color. *Apparently they weren't digitally altered,* she thought, recalling the online photographs she'd viewed.

"Do you wear tinted contact lenses?" The question just popped out of her mouth, and she regretted it the moment she uttered the words.

"Excuse me?" Brady asked, sounding somewhat bemused.

"I'm sorry," Ella said, now embarrassed. "But you really have amazing eyes. I'm sure people tell you that all the time. When I looked you up on the Internet, I wondered if the photographs had been doctored to bring out the color. But looking at them in person, I just wondered if you wore tinted lenses. I'm sorry, that was a rude question."

Brady noticed the blush coloring Ella's face. He studied her features a moment before responding.

"No, I don't wear contacts at all." He resisted the temptation to brush the side of her face with his fingertips. He found it ironic that a woman with such striking eyes herself would notice his eye color.

Of course, she was not the first person to ask the question about tinted contact lenses. One of the scandal rags devoted an entire page to his eye color;

including false claims from an undisclosed optometrist that discussed his imaginary tinted lenses in ridiculous detail. One article even claimed his eye color had been chemically altered. However, all anyone needed to do was look at his mother's eyes, which were the same color. Unfortunately, she had died long before her son became famous.

Studying Ella, Brady found her eyes more compelling than his. Hers were an unusual shade of blue-green, thickly lashed, and from the close proximity, he was fairly certain she wore no makeup. He was used to women concealing their true looks behind a heavy coat of artificial color, and as best as he could tell, Ella Lewis was practically bare; her face, at least. *This is what natural beauty looks like*, he told himself.

Ella wasn't the most beautiful woman he'd ever seen. That would be a ridiculous claim, considering many of those in his social circle were among the most famously beautiful women in the world. This sudden and unexpected attraction toward his rescuer wasn't simply because she was an attractive woman—there was something else. He didn't understand it, but he wanted to explore the attraction.

Ella turned abruptly and walked to a doorway across the hall from the spare bedroom. It was the first time Brady noticed she had a key in her hand. Hastily, Ella unlocked the door. She clutched the doorknob and opened the door slightly. She turned to face Brady.

"You coming?"

Brady walked toward the doorway. When she opened it a bit more, he could see a staircase.

"That takes you to the attic?" he asked, already knowing the answer. Surprised to see the staircase, Brady had expected to get into the attic using a ladder and scuttle hole.

"Yeah. It's probably dusty, but there shouldn't be many spiders, I have this place sprayed four times a year." Ella reached into the dark hallway beyond the door and flipped a switch, turning on an overhead light.

Brady followed her slowly up the narrow wooden staircase. "You were going to tell me why this place freaked you out."

"This cabin used to belong to my parents. I purchased it last year," Ella explained, as she continued up the steps. "My folks rarely went into the attic, but my cousin used to tell me people lived up here, and at night they would come downstairs when we slept. When the cabin would creak late at night, I thought it was the people in the attic."

"That would sure as hell creep a kid out!" Brady laughed.

Ella reached the top of the staircase, where there was a second door. It was unlocked. She opened the door, pushing it in slowly as if she was afraid of what she might find. By her hesitation and body language, Brady suspected some real childhood fear lingered on, and she wasn't teasing when she said the attic freaked her out. Without hesitation, he pushed past her, and opened the door the rest of the way. It was dark in the attic. It took him just a second to find the light switch along the wall next to the doorway. He flipped it on.

A golden glow from a light fixture on the ceiling illuminated the attic room. Glancing around, with Ella behind him at the top of the staircase, he was surprised to discover the space had only a thin layer of dust, and there was no evidence of spider webs. The center portion of the room was tall enough to stand upright, but the slanting ceiling made two of the exterior walls about four feet high. Even with the slanting walls, the space would make a cozy fourth bedroom. On the far end wall was a window, covered with foil.

Cardboard boxes lined either side of the small room. Brady noticed the snowshoes immediately; they were on an old oak dresser on the other side of the room.

"All's clear," Brady said cheerfully, his voice teasing.

"Oh, shut up!" Ella laughed, feeling suddenly foolish for her phobia. Without thinking, she gave his arm a playful punch.

"Ouch!" Brady cried out, exaggerating the pain.

He rubbed his arm and flashed Ella a pouty expression, but the twinkle in his eyes spoiled the effect he was trying to achieve. After a second, he gave Ella a little wink and smile, then walked farther into the room, looking over the numerous boxes.

"So, what's all this stuff?" Brady asked.

"Oh, some of these were up here when I bought the cabin from my folks," Ella explained as she made her way over to the dresser and the snowshoes. "After I decided to rent out the cabin part of the year, I boxed up some of our personal belongings and put them up here. I took some other stuff home. Sometimes I regret renting out the cabin during part of the year, because that means I can't just leave my clothes, toothbrush or food in the pantry. But some of the things, like snowshoes, I just leave up here. The snowshoes are pretty old but they still work." She held up one set for him to see. "I've been considering getting one of the newer pairs; I guess they're easier to walk in. But these will work. I figure where your car is, we should be able to get there in about thirty minutes or so."

"Where is the shoe part of the snowshoe?" Brady asked, reaching out and taking one snowshoe from Ella. He turned the oval shaped object in his hand, noting the animal hide lacing woven on the wooden frame. In its center were leather straps.

"It fastens to your shoe with this," Ella explained,

pointing to the leather straps in the center of the contraption.

"Are there poles?"

"Sorry, I don't have any. I know a lot of people use poles with snowshoes, but I never have. I don't think you'll have a problem. The walk to the Jeep is fairly level."

"One thing I learned today," Brady told her, "my shoes aren't waterproof."

"Well, we'll have to make do with what we have. They should be dry by morning and we can always wrap them in kitchen trash bags before tying them on the snowshoes, to help keep the water out," Ella suggested.

"That's okay, I'll deal with it. I think I'll skip the trash bags," Brady told her, thinking the paparazzi would love to catch him stumbling through the snow wearing an archaic set of snowshoes, his boots covered with trash bags. Ella just shrugged at his reaction and handed him the other snowshoe.

Brady watched as Ella looked through the various boxes. In one, she found several ski gloves, and asked him to try a pair on. He put the snowshoes back on the dresser with the second pair and took the gloves. They fit.

In another box, Ella found several pairs of boots more suitable for snowshoes than Brady's. Sitting on the floor of the attic, Brady tried some on. One pair was about a half-size larger than he normally wore, but with an extra pair of socks, they should work. Fortunately, they discovered wool socks in the bottom of the boot box.

"You know, this room would make a great spare bedroom or office for you," Brady told her, as he tugged off the boots he was planning to wear with the snowshoes.

"I know. I've been considering fixing it up," Ella told him as she closed the box she was rummaging through.

"What's preventing you? Is it your childhood fear?"

"Actually, it would help me dispel that silly fear. No longer would this be some spooky dark storage room. The reason I haven't done anything with this space…. Where do I put all this junk?"

"You have a garage," he reminded her.

"Yeah, but when I rent out the cabin, my tenants can get into the garage, but I can lock the attic," Ella explained as she moved several boxes from the back wall, searching for something. Suddenly she called out, "I found it!'

Brady watched Ella pick up a small sled.

"I was afraid I got rid of the sled," she explained, shoving the boxes back in place. "I thought I set it by the dresser. But I must have shoved it back there before I moved those boxes up here."

She set the sled by Brady, in the middle of the attic floor. Next to him were the boots they'd found, along with several pairs of socks and the ski gloves. Ella leaned down and picked up the socks and gloves, then shoved them into the boots. She grabbed the snowshoes, holding both sets in her arms.

"Can you get the sled and boots, and I'll take these?"

"Sure." Brady stood up from the floor. Ella left the attic first, followed by Brady who turned off the light as he stepped from the room. After walking down the stairs, Ella moved into the hallway and placed the snowshoes on the floor by the door leading to the attic. Brady put the sled and boots next to the snow-shoes, turned off the light in the small hallway, and shut the attic door.

"Do you want to lock this again?"

"I guess so." Taking the key from her pocket, she stepped to the closed door. "I can't have those people from the attic sneaking into my room in the middle of the night."

Brady laughed, yet couldn't help but wonder what Ella would think if he snuck into her room in the middle of the night. As soon as the thought popped into his head, another image flashed, that of the uninvited blonde whom he found in his hotel room bed just days before. Brady cringed inwardly, telling himself that in spite of his earlier suspicions of Ella's intentions toward him, she had done nothing to infer she would welcome his advances.

"You want me to take this stuff downstairs?"

Brady asked as he watched her lock the door. He tried to get the notion of seducing his hostess out of his head.

"That would be great," Ella said as she turned to face him, tucking the key in her pocket. "I'm going to take that shower now. If you're hungry or thirsty, help yourself to anything in the kitchen. I brought a box of wine; feel free to open it if you want something to drink."

"Thanks, Ella."

"No problem." She smiled.

Standing at the end of the hallway, he watched her go into the bedroom and shut the door. Once again, he heard the clicking sound, and knew she had locked her bedroom door. He wondered briefly if she was protecting herself from the imaginary people in the attic, or from him.

Brady leaned down, picked up the snowshoes, and headed downstairs. He would have to make a second trip for the sled and boots.

CHAPTER NINE

*B*rady put the boots in the downstairs bedroom, and set the sled and snowshoes in the garage. Sam was no longer sleeping by the fire, and followed Brady down the hallway to the garage, then back to the kitchen.

In the kitchen, Brady helped himself to a glass of merlot after retrieving the wine box from the pantry. While opening the box, he chuckled to himself, thinking of the expensive case of wine and imported beer Kevin had placed in the back of the Jeep for Brady to take to the cabin. Maybe Brady wasn't a big drinker, but when he did enjoy alcohol, it was normally the best and the most expensive. After a sip of the wine, he had to admit it didn't taste bad.

Sitting on the couch in front of the fire, Brady watched the flames dance in the stone fireplace. Sam lay down by the side of the couch, close to Brady, and let out a little grunting sound before closing her eyes to take a nap. Brady reached down and patted her head, then took another sip of wine.

He considered the day's events and his behavior toward Ella. He had to admit, had she not come along when she did, he very well might have died in the storm. She had saved his life. As he began replaying the day back in his mind, he couldn't help but experience a surge of embarrassment and regret. *I behaved like an ass*, he told himself. Yawning, he suddenly realized he was exhausted. The day's adventures had kicked his ass.

Downing his wine in record time, he set the empty glass on the coffee table, pulled his feet onto the couch and tucked one of the sofa's throw pillows under his head. Within minutes, he was fast asleep.

When Brady woke from his nap, the first thing he observed was a darkened room lit only by the warm glow from the fireplace. Sitting up on the couch and placing his bare feet on the floor, he noticed he'd been covered while he slept. It was the same quilt he'd used earlier and left folded in the laundry room. Obviously, Ella was responsible. Brady smiled at the considerate gesture. It appeared he was alone downstairs; even Sam was nowhere in sight. The fire still raged, and he suspected Ella had fed the flames while he napped.

Groggily getting up from the couch and wondering how long he had slept, Brady combed his fingers through his dark hair. Letting the quilt fall from his lap to the floor, he stretched for a moment. He reached down, picked the quilt off the floor and tossed it to the couch before heading to the kitchen.

There were no lights on downstairs, and he wondered what Ella was doing. Resisting the temptation to go upstairs and check, he walked into the kitchen and turned on the lights. The kitchen was illuminated for just a few seconds before he was plunged back into darkness. Reaching for the light switch again, he flipped it several times. Nothing happened.

A few moments later, he heard Ella noisily coming down the staircase, Sam trailing after her.

"Damn electricity has gone out," Ella cursed as she walked into the kitchen carrying her flashlight.

"How long does it usually stay off when this happens?" Brady asked.

"It usually goes back on in a couple of hours, but this is a bad storm, so I don't expect it to come on until morning. I tried the phone upstairs earlier, and it's still down. Did you have a good sleep? You've been out for hours."

"Yes, I did. Thanks for the blanket."

"No problem. You hungry?"

"Yes, a little. What've you been doing? Did you take a nap?"

"No, I never nap. If I sleep during the day, it wipes me out. I might as well stay in bed until the next day. I was working. I was on a roll when the damn electricity went out. I was tempted to keep writing in the dark until my laptop battery dies, but I'm kind of hungry."

Ella opened the refrigerator and shined her flashlight inside. Brady watched as she grabbed food from the refrigerator, and then more items from the pantry.

"I wanted to apologize," Brady began, silently watching Ella in the poorly lit room.

She paused a moment and glanced over at Brady. Light from the fireplace illuminated his features with a golden glow.

"Apologize?" Ella asked.

"If it wasn't for you, I'd still be in the snow, most likely dead. I behaved like an ass, beginning with cutting you off at the gas station."

"Oh, that." Ella chuckled. "Do you normally cut people off at the gas pumps?" She sounded as if she was teasing, but she was genuinely curious.

"To be honest, I haven't driven a car in years," Brady confessed. "The Jeep belongs to Kevin."

"Are you serious?" Ella found that hard to believe.

"We have a limo with a driver, and since I've been living in one hotel after another during the last five years, there really has been no reason for me to drive."

"I thought you rock stars lived in fancy motor homes when on the road."

"Please don't call me a rock star," he asked. "I've never been much for homes on wheels." He thought about the crappy trailers he'd lived in growing up.

"Hotels are better?" Ella asked.

"They have room service, clean sheets and I never have to buy soap or shampoo."

"I would hate not having my own place."

As they chatted, she arranged food on a tray. Since there was no electricity, she would not be able to cook dinner. Instead, they would feast on finger food consisting of cheese, deli meats, fruit and hard rolls. She picked up the tray and told Brady to follow her into the living room.

She set the tray on the coffee table and sat on the couch. Brady picked his empty wine glass up from the table.

"Want me to get you a glass of wine?" Brady offered.

"That would be great. I was so hungry, I forgot about the wine."

Moments later, Brady returned to the couch carrying two glasses of merlot. He sat with Ella on the couch, while the two ate from the tray. Sam suddenly appeared, obviously hoping for a hand-out. Ella pointed away from the couch and told Sam to go lay down. Reluctantly, the dog moved away from the tray of food and lay down on the floor, resigned to the fact she was not invited to the indoor picnic.

"I take it this is your vacation cabin. Where do you normally live?"

"Canyon City."

"Where we had breakfast?" Brady asked. He then remembered the man from the gas station had mentioned that.

"Yes, I've a condo there. I loved your wig by the way," Ella added with a giggle, unable to resist commenting. She remembered how silly he looked sitting in the restaurant booth wearing the odd hairpiece. Brady groaned, and then laughed before taking a sip of wine.

"No you didn't." He laughed. "You fairly ripped it from my head when I got in your car."

"Why in the world did you have it on? I understood the restaurant; you were trying to hide your identity. But why wear it out in a snowstorm?"

"I didn't have a hat," he explained.

"Well, that makes more sense. I wish I'd taken a picture when I found you stumbling down the road with the wig on. I betcha I could've sold that picture for big bucks to one of those scandal sheets."

"I'm sure you could have," Brady agreed with a chuckle.

"So, did you really come here to get away from fans and paparazzi?" Ella popped a piece of cheese into her mouth.

"Yes. They're one reason I had to get a limo and hire a driver. If I was allowed to drive, I would've hit one of those jerks by now, and would probably be in prison today."

"I wouldn't like that, the annoying paparazzi always snapping my picture."

"Neither do I." Brady leaned back on the couch and propped his bare feet on the coffee table. "But it's part of the job."

"Are fans as annoying?" Ella asked.

"I don't want to say anything bad about my fans. If it wasn't for them, I wouldn't have all that I do. But unfortunately, some get a little out of control. For example, the other day I returned to my hotel room to discover a nude woman in my bed."

"Was she ugly?" Ella asked.

"No, actually she was pretty hot. Why would you ask if she was ugly?"

"Well, guys I know would be thrilled to find a naked chick in their bed, unless of course there was something wrong with her."

"Would you be upset if you frequently came home to discover strange nude men waiting in your bed?"

Ella almost gave the flip reply: *if he was hot it would be cool.* The truth was, she would be horrified to find a nude stranger in her bed, and it wouldn't matter how good looking he was.

"I see what you mean. It's just that I always hear stories about rock…I mean people in your profession, and how having sex with groupies is just part of the life."

"Having indiscriminate sex with strangers can kill you," Brady reminded her.

"You're right," Ella sat her wine glass on the table and stood up. She walked to the fireplace, pulled a log off the rack, and tossed it in the flames.

"That's one reason I'm grateful to be able to make a living with my writing, and why I have no desire to become a well-known bestselling author. Not that bestselling authors usually find nude people in their beds, but their fans can still be intrusive."

"According to the guy at the gas station you write romance. You can actually make a living without being considered a bestselling author?"

"Historical romance," Ella clarified as she returned to the couch and sat down. "Compared to what traditionally published mid-list authors made before eBooks and self-publishing took off, I probably make more. It's a comfortable living, but I'm not rich and famous. Rich I would like, famous not so much."

"Why not famous?" He remembered how hungry he had been for the fame along with the money. Looking back, he had wanted fame more.

"I've a writer friend who started self-publishing about the same time as me. Her first book took off immediately. It shot to the top of the charts and made the New York Times Bestseller List. For years, she had been trying to get an agent and publisher, and suddenly she has agent's knocking on her door. They made her a sweet deal, and her second and third book did even better than the first. She made appearances on all the talk shows, and overnight she had strangers knocking on her front door, showing up at her kid's private school to snap a picture of her picking him up. She ended up moving two times the first year, trying to get some privacy."

"I can definitely relate."

"Don't get me wrong, she's happy with her life, and doesn't complain about her loss of privacy, but I don't think I could handle it as well as she does."

"What do you plan to do if your next book makes it to the bestseller list?" he asked.

"Well, I write under a pen name, whereas my friend used her real name. Hopefully I'll be able to keep my true identity a secret if that ever happens."

"The guy at the gas station knows who you are, so it really isn't a secret now."

"Yeah, I suppose you're right there. It's a small town, and my friends all know what I write. My pen name is not exactly a secret. I don't have my real name on my website, or on my Facebook author's page. Of course, it's mentioned on my personal Facebook page, but only friends see that. Hopefully, if I'm ever so lucky to make it to the New York Times Bestseller List, my friends will respect my privacy. Don't get me wrong; it's not that I'm afraid of success. I'd love for my titles to make it to the top of the charts. I want readers to love my books. I don't necessarily want them to love me."

Ella sipped her wine and considered some of Brady's earlier comments when he seemed to assume she was some obsessed fan who had followed him to the mountain. Remembering some of the stories her writer friend had told her involving overeager fans, she understood better why he behaved in such a manner. Ella couldn't help but feel a little sorry for him. She would not want his life.

They talked for another twenty minutes when Ella finally said, "I think I'll head back upstairs and get more writing done before I get to bed. I figure I have at least three hours on the laptop battery before it goes out."

Fifteen minutes later, Brady found himself once again alone in front of the fireplace. Even Sam had abandoned him, going upstairs with Ella instead of staying by the warmth of the fire.

Staring into the flames, Brady contemplated the unusual set of circumstances. Last week, had he known he would be stranded in a blizzard with a beautiful young woman, he would never imagine she would choose to work upstairs on her computer instead of staying with him by the warmth of a fire during an electrical outage. What surprised him most was the fact he wished she'd stayed downstairs with him.

CHAPTER TEN

$\mathcal{T}$he inviting aroma of coffee woke Brady the next morning. Sleepily, he opened his eyes and looked around the unfamiliar bedroom. For a moment, he forgot where he was. Then he remembered —the blizzard, Ella. Stretching beneath the pile of warm quilts, Brady delayed getting from bed, enjoying the surrounding comfort. Breathing in the scent of freshly brewed coffee, he remembered the electrical outage.

"I guess the electricity is back on," he said aloud to the empty room; then smiled, thinking how he'd enjoy some crisp bacon, and recalled seeing a package in the refrigerator.

Pulling back the covers, Brady's bare skin felt the frigid nip of the air. He was surprised at how chilly it was in the room. The only thing he wore were boxers, so he quickly got from the bed and redressed in the same clothes he'd worn the day before, which he'd left on a chair on the other side of the room. He grabbed the wool socks Ella had given him and hastily tugged them onto his feet.

Walking to the bedroom window, he looked outside. It was impossible to tell where the side yard ended and the street began. White covered everything, but the sun was shining and a few clouds remained in the sky. Brady didn't know if it was the beginning of a new storm, or the remnants of yesterday's blizzard.

Still chilly, even with clothes on, he left the room and headed toward the kitchen and living room area. He found Ella sitting at the breakfast bar, drinking a cup of coffee.

"Good morning," Ella said brightly. "I hope you slept okay. Would you like a cup of coffee?"

"I'd love one. Can we turn the heater up? It's kind of cold in here," Brady asked as he crossed his arms over his chest and rubbed each of his forearms with an opposing hand.

"Sorry, but the power's still off. I'm afraid the fire was about out when I got up this morning, but I've added some logs, so it should warm up. Unfortunately, fireplaces don't really add that much heat. Times like this I wish I had a woodstove. Much better for heating."

She stood up, walked into the kitchen area and

grabbed a second coffee mug from the overhead cupboard.

"Then how did you make the coffee?"

Ella answered by pointing to the fireplace. Brady looked in that direction and saw the blue enamel camping coffee pot sitting on a brick in the fireplace, next to the flickering flames.

"I also dug out my Dutch oven this morning. I had it shoved to the back of a cupboard. I figure we can use that to heat up the chili, or cook other meals, for as long as this power stays off," Ella explained while she walked to the fireplace with the empty mug. Bending down by the stone hearth, she used one of the brass fireplace tools to drag the coffee pot closer to her, and away from the flames. Using a potholder she'd left on the hearth, she grabbed hold of the pot's handle. After pouring a cup of coffee, she set the pot back in the fireplace and handed the hot mug to Brady.

"Do you use cream or sugar? I don't have cream, but I have milk."

"No, black is fine." Brady gratefully accepted the mug and started to take a sip, but it was scalding, so he gently blew on the hot liquid, waiting for it to cool before taking another.

"You'll have to excuse the coffee grinds," Ella said, grabbing her mug from the counter and sitting back on a barstool. "I'm afraid it is a bit… rustic."

Brady finally tasted the coffee and winced.

"Umm, it's also pretty strong. I think I will take some of that milk."

"Well, you'll find it in the cooler over on the counter. This morning I took some of the perishables from the refrigerator and packed them in the cooler with blue ice I had in the freezer. Later, if necessary, we can use snow. While the refrigerator is still cold, I'm a little concerned about spoilage, and if we are stuck here for a few days, the idea of eating just canned food does not thrill me."

Brady helped himself to some of the milk in the ice chest, adding a splash to his coffee. After returning the carton of milk to the cooler and replacing the cooler's lid, he joined Ella at the break-fast bar.

"It tastes good, coffee grinds and all," Brady told her as he took another sip.

"Yeah, coffee is a morning necessity. If we didn't have a fireplace, you'd find me outside making a campfire. Or in my snowshoes, heading to town for a cup at the diner."

"About those snowshoes, do you think we'll be able to get my things from the Jeep?"

"Yes, but I think we should do it this morning. I really don't like the looks of those clouds. I have a feeling we're going to be in for an afternoon storm, and I'd rather be back here before it hits. Hey, where are the keys to your Jeep?"

"I think I left them in the ignition, why?"

"Well, maybe we can get it unstuck and you can drive it back here. That way you can try to make it to your rental cabin when it's safe or even head off the mountain if this isn't the kind of getaway you were planning."

"My only problem," Brady began, feeling embarrassed. "I can't remember how to put it in four-wheel drive. That's why I got stuck in the first place."

"You don't know how to put your Jeep in four-wheel drive?" she asked, sounding incredulous.

"Remember, it isn't my Jeep."

"What kind of Jeep is it?"

"A Wrangler," he told her.

"No problem. My old boyfriend had one of those, and we used to go four wheeling. I'm sure I can remember how to put it in four-wheel drive."

"That would be great." Brady took another sip of his coffee and then looked at Ella, studying her expression. She looked out the kitchen window, and he wondered what she was thinking.

"You mention an old boyfriend; do you have a current boyfriend? I don't know why, but I assumed you weren't married. You aren't, are you?"

Ella laughed at his question. "No, no husband. I almost made it to the altar once, right out of college. How about you? When I looked you up on the Internet, I saw no mention of a wife or girlfriend. Yet, lots of pictures with you and hot celebrities," Ella said in a teasing voice. She was now looking at Brady instead of out the window.

"I really don't have the time for a relationship," Brady told her.

"I also imagine it must be hard for you," Ella noted, silently considering his situation for a minute.

"What do you mean?" He finished the last of his coffee.

"I don't know, living in hotels, going from one concert to the next. Having naked chicks show up, uninvited in your bed and paparazzi snapping your picture at every turn. If you did find someone you wanted to start a relationship with, it wouldn't be easy with all that going on." Ella shook her head, as if she couldn't imagine such a life. Brady suddenly realized she felt sorry for him.

"So what about you, have a current boyfriend?" After asking the question, Brady stood up from the barstool and walked to the fireplace to help himself to another cup of coffee. On his way there, he snatched Ella's almost empty mug and took it with him to refill. Ella turned around in the barstool so she could watch Brady.

"No. I dated my last boyfriend for about a year. We broke it off about a month ago."

"How come?" Brady asked while bending down by the hearth and pouring the coffee.

"Aren't you nosey?" Ella laughed.

Brady just smiled and waited for her answer.

"Oh, I don't know. He was a nice enough guy. But it really wasn't meant to be. Plus, I caught him in bed with another woman."

By her tone, she didn't seem upset, or if she had been upset at the time, she appeared to be over the breakup.

"Maybe it wasn't his fault. Maybe he came home and found her in his bed. That does happen." He walked back to the breakfast bar and handed Ella her mug. Ella noted the mischievous twinkle in his eyes. She started to giggle.

"Um, I don't think so. For one thing, it was the woman's bed, not his. Yet, now that you mention it, the scenario wasn't all that different than what you describe. The main difference, you kicked her out. You did kick her out?"

"The blonde? Yes, or rather my bodyguards removed her. So tell me, how was it similar?"

"She was someone who I thought was a friend. She called me one morning and asked me if I could come over for lunch. Told me there was something she really needed to talk to me about and it couldn't wait. I'm naturally curious, so I agreed. She told me she was repapering her bedroom, so to let myself in when I got there and go on into her bedroom."

"Oh, no, are you saying..." Brady moaned, already knowing where this was going.

"Yep. I walked into her bedroom, and there she was with my boyfriend. Both of them buck naked, rolling around on her sheets. If you think my expression was utter horror, you should've seen his. It was obvious he had no idea I was on the guest list. When I think about it, I should have realized something was off when she mentioned she was repapering her bedroom. Who wallpapers these days?" Ella laughed.

"Why did she do it? Aside from the fact she's a bitch."

"Well, I stormed out before anyone said anything. Craig showed up at my house that afternoon, pleading with me. He insisted she'd ask him over under some innocent pretense. I don't recall what it was—who knows, maybe to look at her plumbing or something. According to him, she seduced him, and him being a red-blooded man, how could he resist? He insisted it had nothing to do with how he felt about me. Insisted he loved me."

"So why did she do it? Did you ever find out?"

"I always knew she was a little…eccentric. And I'm sure it happen just as he described. As for why, I imagine she wanted him and figured it was a way to kill two birds with one stone. It would break us up, while push him into her arms."

"Is he still seeing her?"

"According to my friends, no. Craig tried calling me a few times after that, asking me to forgive him. He finally stopped calling when I pointed out, not only did the episode prove he wasn't committed to our relationship, the fact I got over the breakup relatively quickly, showed I wasn't committed either. Perhaps she did me a favor."

"I feel a little sorry for the guy."

"Why? You kicked the blonde out of your bed, and you didn't even have a girlfriend."

"That's true, Ella, but she was not the first blonde that showed up in my bed. I wasn't so noble the first time it happened. So I do understand the temptation your boyfriend felt."

"Hey! You can't take my ex-boyfriend's side in this! You have to be on my side!" Ella exclaimed with mock outrage.

"Why? Don't guys have to stick together?"

"Not when I'm the one with the warm—semi-warm—cabin, hot coffee and food. Before you answer, remember how cold it is outside."

"Okay, okay!" Brady laughed, "That guy was a major douche!"

"That's better!" Ella said with a smile, and then stood up. "How about we have some breakfast then head to the Jeep before the clouds get any worse."

"I confess I woke up thinking of bacon this morning, but I don't imagine that's going to happen," Brady said with a sigh.

"Sorry. Maybe if I wasn't anxious to get out of here early, I'd try cooking some in the Dutch oven. Maybe tomorrow morning. And who knows, the electricity may be on by then."

"What can I help you with?" Brady asked.

"Nothing exciting for breakfast, just cold cereal and juice. Sorry."

"You know what they say."

"What's that?" Ella grabbed two boxes of cereal from the pantry.

"Beggars can't be choosers."

"How true!" Ella agreed, still smiling.

She offered Brady his choice of Cheerios or generic shredded wheat. He took Cheerios. Ella scolded him when he spooned sugar over it.

"That stuff will kill you," she warned.

"Then why did you buy it?" he asked before he shoveled a spoonful of sweetened cereal into his mouth.

"It has its place. Just not on your cereal."

"Coffee?" Brady asked.

"Oh, never coffee. The only thing you should ever put in coffee is milk or cream."

"You're pretty opinionated," he teased.

"Of course not. Opinions have nothing to do with it. I'm just right. That's all," she playfully insisted.

Sitting side by side at the counter, they ate their breakfast of cereal, orange juice and coffee. Brady silently considered the fact that yesterday at this time they were strangers, having breakfast at the same diner, at separate booths. He found it difficult to believe that less than 24 hours ago he had imagined she was some deranged fan who'd followed him up to the mountain to insinuate herself into his life.

Meeting Ella was like stepping back in time, before his career, when no one aside from his small circle of family and friends knew who he was. While his childhood was not a period he enjoyed reflecting on, it was not all bad. When he was in junior high school, he and his mother lived in a trailer park. It was one of the three trailer parks they stayed at during his adolescent years. In that particular park, a girl name Melissa had lived next door. They were the same age and she had been his best friend.

Talking with Ella reminded Brady of Melissa. He never imagined he would feel that sense of ease with a female ever again. To Melissa, he was just regular old Brady, her pal and buddy. He wasn't yet a famous rock star whose picture regularly appeared in the scandal sheets and celebrity magazines. Until this time with Ella, Brady hadn't realized how much he missed this—enjoying a woman's company without his celebrity coloring the moment.

CHAPTER ELEVEN

"Craig left this in my closet the last time we were here." Ella handed Brady a plush ski jacket. He stood in the downstairs hallway wearing the clothes he'd worn the day before, along with two pairs of wool socks from the attic and the borrowed boots and gloves. "I think it'll fit, and will be much warmer than what you have on. There's also a knit hat in the pocket."

Brady took the jacket and slipped it on after removing his own coat. It fit perfectly and it was much warmer than his was. Taking the hat from the pocket, he hesitated a moment and just looked at it.

"Oh, don't worry," Ella said with a laugh. "That's one of mine, and I promise it's clean. No lice."

Brady smiled at Ella, then slipped the knit cap on his head and down over his ears.

"Plus," Ella added, "it works much better than the blond wig."

Brady chuckled and followed Ella to the garage, where the snowshoes waited. His gaze fixed on her backside.

Her snug black ski pants hugged her curves, leaving little to the imagination. Under her pink parka, she wore a pink and orange-striped turtleneck sweater. The ends of her blonde-streaked hair peeked out from under a white knit cap. Brady thought she looked incredibly sexy in the outfit, but withheld comment. Her boots, covered in faux fur, were more stylish than the old ones he wore.

Sam tried to follow them into the garage, but Ella made her stay in the house.

"She isn't going?" Brady asked.

"No, I really don't want to end up bringing her back in the sled. Walking in the snow, even for a dog, can be tiring, especially for one like Sam, with leg issues."

Once in the garage, they closed the door behind them to keep Sam inside. Ella pressed the control to the automatic garage door opener. Nothing happened.

"I think that needs electricity to run," Brady teased.

"Oh, yeah, that was pretty lame of me," Ella grumbled, feeling embarrassed. She walked to the other end of the garage, pulled the red handle hanging from the ceiling to release the automatic opener, and then manually pulled the double garage door up and open.

Brady was about to ask if she needed help, but she had the door open before he made his offer.

"I think I'll leave it open while we're gone. I'm not really concerned about someone breaking in. And coming and going will be easier for us if the door is open, especially with the sled."

Ella picked up the sled and set it outside on the snow, just beyond the garage door opening. A red rope was attached to the front of the sled. Brady hadn't noticed the rope before, and assumed Ella must have added it sometime that morning.

Along one inside wall of the garage was a bench. Ella told Brady to sit there. After he was sitting, she knelt before him and began fastening one snowshoe onto his right boot. Brady looked down at the top of Ella's head. Her attention was focused solely on fastening his boot. Seeing her kneeling before him, indecent and carnal thoughts flashed through his mind. He shifted restlessly on the bench.

"Hold still," Ella scolded, without looking up. Brady closed his eyes briefly and prayed she keep her attention fixed to his feet. He moved his arms, awkwardly covering his lap, to prevent Ella from noticing his body's response. The fact the ski jacket was already covering the area did not make Brady feel any better, and he told himself he needed to stop having those thoughts about his host.

After she secured the first snowshoe, she fastened the second. She sat down on the bench, next to Brady, and put on her own snowshoes. She failed to notice how quiet he had become.

Ella stood up and walked toward the garage door opening. She waddled slightly; keeping her feet widely spaced, to prevent one snowshoe from stepping on the other one. Brady was so fascinated by her interesting waddle that he followed her without paying attention to the placement of his own feet. He soon learned the error of his way when he landed the right snowshoe on his left, sending him lurching forward straight into Ella.

She had just stepped onto the snow covered driveway when Brady came tumbling into her, landing them both outside, sprawled on the frozen snow. Ella landed face first with the deep cold powder cushioning her landing. It wasn't the initial fall that caused her to let out an unfeminine grunt; it was Brady's body landing atop her, slamming his weight into hers, sending her deeper in the snow.

He immediately rolled to one side, off her body. Once he realized he hadn't inflicted any real damage, he regretted his hasty departure and wished he could enjoy a few minutes with Ella under him. She felt good there and while having sex in the snow might freeze off some vital body parts, he found the idea intriguing.

"What the hell?" Ella cursed, rolling to one side, away from Brady, while trying to sit up. She brushed the snow off her face and the front of her jacket.

"I'm really sorry, Ella. I tripped," Brady told her. He managed to get to his feet first, and extended his hand to help her up. She accepted his gloved hand and awkwardly stood up. Miraculously, the snow-shoes were still attached.

"I guess that was my fault," Ella told him, sounding apologetic. She continued to brush snow off her clothing.

"Your fault?" Brady was surprised she wasn't furious with him.

"I should've warned you," Ella explained. "You need to keep your feet slightly apart, or…or what just happened will happen again. Be careful not to step on your own snowshoe. It's fairly easy to walk in them, but you need to pay attention and take deliberate steps."

Ella clomped her way to the sled and picked up the red rope. "I'll pull this," she told him. "You just concentrate on staying upright. When you walk and place one foot on the ground, keep the toe up a bit. You don't want to put the toe down first. That can make you stumble."

Instead of walking down the driveway, Ella made

a wide turn and walked toward her backyard, pulling the sled behind her. Brady followed, keeping a safe distance from Ella, not wanting to further embarrass himself by knocking her down again. Focusing his attention on every step he took, Brady didn't have the luxury to admire Ella's backside as they walked out from her backyard, cutting through the woods.

The first thing he noticed, once he fell into a comfortable stride, was the lack of sound. Occasionally, snow would fall from a tree limb and break the silence. The air was frigid on his face, and his nose was cold, but fortunately, the rest of his body was comfortably warm.

"It's beautiful out here," Brady said at last. Ella stopped walking and turned to face him, smiling.

"It is, isn't it?" She paused for just a moment, before starting back on her trek.

Surrounded by pine trees, Ella's cabin was no longer in sight. Brady spied several other cabins in the distance. At one point, they crossed over a road and back into the wooded area, but Brady didn't notice, because everything was covered in snow. It was impossible to tell where a road began and the wilderness ended.

With his breathing slightly labored from the exertion, Brady tried his best to keep pace with Ella, who seemed quite at ease on the snowshoes. While traipsing through the mountains after a blizzard wasn't on his to-do list when he planned this getaway, he had to admit he was enjoying himself. He loved the fact no one was following him. No one was watching him. If he fell on his ass again—or on Ella's—no one would be snapping and tweeting his picture. He also loved the fact Ella was treating him like a person—not a *rock star*. Until he met Ella, he never hated the moniker *rock star*.

It took almost forty-five minutes, instead of thirty, to reach the Jeep. Brady was relieved when it finally came into view. Ella had offered to stop several times so he might rest, yet Brady always responded, *don't stop for me. I am okay if you are.* When they finally reached the Jeep, he told himself he needed to drop the macho routine, and the next time Ella asked if he needed a rest, he would say *yes.*

Much of the snow along the driver's side of the Jeep had already melted by the time they reached it, due to the angle of the car in the ditch and the direction of the morning sun. It was necessary to remove their snowshoes before clearing away enough snow to gain access to the door on the driver's side and the rear hatch. Brady was grateful for the waterproof ski gloves, which enabled him to shovel snow without getting his hands wet.

One of the first things Ella noticed was that the door was not shut all the way. She opened it and sat down sideways on the driver's seat while Brady stood beside the vehicle.

"The keys are in the ignition!" she told him.

The next moment, he heard her curse.

"What's wrong?"

"The battery is dead. We won't be driving it back, sorry."

Brady realized he wasn't upset over the dead battery. If the car worked, it meant they could drive back to the cabin instead of walk, which he wouldn't mind. Yet, it also meant it would be easier for him to leave Ella's cabin.

Ella turned around in the seat to reach the suitcase. It was open, so she re-zipped it before pulling it from the backseat and handing it to Brady. He took the piece of luggage and set it on the sled.

"There's some boxes in the back, do you want them? I think we have room," Ella told him. She looked around the front and back seat, and saw nothing else. *He travels light*, she told herself.

"Kevin thought I would need that," Brady said with a chuckle. "It's some beer and wine. We don't have to take them."

"The hell we don't! Are you insane, man? Who knows how long we may be stuck in the mountains! We need it for medicinal purposes, doncha know. It could save our lives!" Ella handed Brady the keys so he could open the back of the Jeep. He couldn't help but laugh at her.

While everything fit on the sled, Brady wondered how they were going to keep it from falling off. Before he could voice his concerns, Ella was standing at his side and pulling a long rope from her parka's pocket.

"What are you, a Girl Scout?" He watched as Ella quickly tied the items securely to the sled.

"I like to be prepared." She didn't ask for his help, and obviously didn't need it.

"I guess you do. Lucky for me. Maybe I should hire you as my bodyguard instead of Kevin."

"Ha! You couldn't afford me!" Ella laughed. After she secured the items on the sled, she helped Brady put his snowshoes back on, before putting on hers.

Brady insisted on pulling the sled back to the cabin, telling Ella it was only fair. Since Brady seemed to have mastered the snowshoes, she didn't argue. Together they trudged back to her cabin. Overhead, the sky darkened.

"I think it's a good thing we did this early," Ella noted, glancing up to the sky. She found herself breathing a little heavily, getting tired from the outing.

"I think you're right. It looks nasty. After yesterday, I really don't want to be stuck out in a blizzard again."

"At least you're dressed for the weather today. Of course, a blizzard can be deadly even if you're dressed properly, considering how easy it is to get lost, even if you're in your own backyard."

"True. I'm starting to get cold. How about you?" Brady asked.

"Not only cold, I'm exhausted. For your first time on snowshoes, you did really good."

"I guess you forgot about my initial launch?" He laughed.

"Oh, that. Not a terrific start, but it all worked out. Another photo opportunity missed. Put that baby up on Youtube, and it would go viral in a matter of minutes!"

"Listen to you! Turning into a paparazzi before my very eyes!" Brady teased.

"Nah, I would never have the heart to follow someone around day in and out and invade their privacy. I don't understand how those people do that."

"In the beginning, it's flattering to be the object of the paparazzi."

"You mean, like a sign that you've made it?"

As they chatted, they continued to steadily plod through the snow with Brady pulling the sled.

"Yes. In the beginning, you welcome all the publicity you can get. You look for it. I can't speak for everyone, but for me, when paparazzi first started camping at my door, I really didn't understand it was not a temporary situation. Maybe a part of me didn't believe my success was going to last, so I expected the paparazzi to just get bored and move onto the next hot topic.

"One day something clicks. I realize—I've truly arrived. It's all real. And you know what, those rude people flashing cameras in my face, day in and out, are not going away. That's when it all started to change for me."

"Change?" Ella asked.

"I guess the best way to describe it. I felt isolated."

"You feel isolated, and your solution is to go alone to a mountain cabin, and stay for several weeks? I won't even mention the looming blizzard part."

"It worked. Today is the first time in years I haven't felt isolated and alone."

"But your plan didn't work out. You never made it to the cabin, and you aren't alone."

"Exactly, Ella. Exactly."

Ella silently considered his words. She stared ahead, and continued to walk, her snowshoes occasionally sticking to ice.

She had to admit she liked this Brady much better than the first one she met. It was almost as if there were two Brady's. The first one was the famous, demanding and narcissistic rock star. He was the one who didn't think twice about cutting her off at the gas pump, accusing her of stalking him, or demanding she risk her life to take him to his cabin. This second Brady was more subdued, slightly vulnerable, and she enjoyed his company. Ella knew that once he returned to his own life, any friendship that might develop would most likely be forgotten.

She understood that he would never have the time to maintain a friendship with someone like her, considering his lifestyle. Plus, she had no desire to step in to his world.

They chatted for the remainder of their walk back to the cabin. Ella was so engrossed in their discussion that she never once asked Brady if he needed to stop and rest. In turn, Brady was so caught up in their conversation that the thought of stopping along the way never occurred to him, either.

It was just starting to snow when they reached Ella's cabin. They hurried into the garage, pulling the sled behind them. Ella let Sam out to do her business, and then she and Brady shed their boots, gloves and jackets, leaving them on the garage bench to dry. Brady helped Ella pull down the garage door before going into the cabin.

CHAPTER TWELVE

One of the first things they noticed when entering the cabin was that the heater was running. The electricity was back on. Ella went immediately to the telephone and picked up the receiver, but the landline was still out.

Instead of using the Dutch oven in the fireplace, Ella put the chili in a stainless steel pan to heat it on the stove. She asked Brady to put some more logs on the fire while she heated lunch. Although they'd eaten breakfast less than three hours before, both were ravenous. Cereal and juice wasn't enough to ward off hunger pangs until noon, not after their morning hike.

"When did you refill the log rack?" Brady asked when he pulled several sticks of firewood from the rack sitting adjacent to the fireplace. It was completely full.

"I did that when I got up this morning. I've a cord of wood outside, and I figured I'd better refill the rack before the snow started again."

"You really are a Girl Scout," he said with a chuckle. Brady tossed the wood on the fire before looking out the window. The snow was now falling at an accelerated rate. White streams of snow on a grey backdrop replaced the once blue, cloud-filled morning sky.

"We made it back just in time," Brady told her, still staring out the window with his back to Ella, who was busy in the kitchen area.

She looked up from what she was doing and gazed across the living room to the large picture window.

"Looks kind of nasty out there. Not saying it isn't pretty, but I'm glad we're in here and not outside."

"Do you need me to help you with lunch?" Brady asked, turning from the window and walking to the breakfast bar.

"No, I think I have everything handled."

"Then I'll bring in the boxes and suitcase from the sled."

Brady brought the boxes of beer and wine into the kitchen, setting them on the counter. Ella teased him about his expensive tastes in beverages, yet she had no clue how much the beer and wine cost. Had she known how expensive they really were, she would have been shocked.

He took the suitcase into the downstairs bedroom, and began to unpack. Anxious to get out of Kevin's pants and shirt, and into something he felt more comfortable in, he changed his clothes before returning to the kitchen.

"For some reason, those clothes look more you," Ella said when he walked into the room. He wore dark slacks and a black pullover sweater. "I think black is your color. Although, I'm not sure it is a color." His slacks were more fitted, and not baggy like the borrowed pair. Ella understood why women found him so attractive. *If he wasn't a rock star, I would so be all over that,* Ella told herself, only half-teasing.

After lunch, Brady offered to help her clean up, and this time she didn't say no. He wasn't as inept in the kitchen as she originally thought, and the two managed to efficiently move around in the small area without getting into each other's way.

Ella made them each a cup of hot green tea, which they enjoyed by the fire, while Sam slept by their feet. The conversation began by recounting their snow-shoe adventure. Brady asked if she snow skied, which led to a story about his water skiing trips before he became famous. The discussion moved to tales of travel, comparing notes on places they'd been, when Ella finally realized they'd been talking for several hours.

"I really need to get upstairs to work on my manuscript, before the power goes out again."

"You think it will?"

Ella stood up from the couch. "Possible. This was fun. But I better get to work."

"Yeah, me too. I'm going to grab my iPad. I promise to use my earphones, so I won't disturb you." Brady stood up and resisted an impulse to kiss her goodbye. Watching Ella walk up the stairs, he wondered briefly if his attraction to her was in part fueled by her seemingly lack of interest in him. He imagined her rushing back downstairs into his arms, and begging him to make love to her. *That would be a great way to spend the rest of the afternoon*, he told himself. Letting out a sigh, he walked to the downstairs guest bedroom.

The two fell into a comfortable routine for the rest of the week. They shared their meals; each participating in the preparation and clean up. Between meals, Ella would go upstairs to write, and Brady would stay downstairs and work on his music. Outside, the snow piled higher, and there were no signs of the snowplow. The phone remained off while the electricity remained on. Each evening, they opened a new bottle of wine and lingered by the fireplace while discussing every topic imaginable.

"You can really make a living self-publishing?" Brady asked one night. The two sat on the floor, leaning against the front of the couch as they faced the fireplace. Sam's head rested on Ella's lap. Absently, Ella stroked the top of the dog's head while she used her other hand to hold the long stemmed wineglass, half-filled with merlot.

"I do alright. Last year, I actually made more than one of my friends who's a teacher. Of course, what they pay teachers, that isn't saying much." Ella laughed, and then took another sip of wine. "Why do you sound so surprised?"

"Oh…" Brady continued to stare into the flames. "A while back I met with a publisher, who was interested in a book deal on my life. She warned me against the independent author, telling me most were hacks."

"Sounds like someone feels threatened by self-publishing upstarts." Ella chuckled. "Yet, not everyone who is doing this is making a living. I know of a number of Indies—some very talented, who feel lucky to sell a couple books a month."

"What's the secret? If you say they're talented, why you and not them, too?"

"I was fortunate to discover a fan base, and they've been really supportive and continue to buy my new books. And, I keep writing. When I publish one, I move onto the next. I have no idea what would happen if I stopped writing. Would my books continue to sell? I'm not getting rich like some successful Indies. For me, it's a decent wage, doing something I love. So I guess I'm blessed."

"What's the process?"

"What do you mean?"

"How does a writer decide to self-publish? I'm curious, how it all works."

"Obviously, it begins by writing something."

"When did you start writing?"

"Do you really want to hear all this?" Ella turned to look at Brady, wondering if he was just being polite. He didn't appear bored, just the opposite.

"Yes, I do. I find it kind of fascinating."

"Well, I've been writing stories since I was a little girl. I was a history major in college, and while I loved history, I always thought the classes were kind of boring. I had a lot of friends that couldn't understand why I was majoring in history. *It is so boring,* they would say. One day I decided to write a story that wasn't boring, yet would also teach the reader something about history. While I write fiction, I try to make the historical settings accurate."

"Did you try the traditional publisher route before self-publishing?"

"After I finished my first book, my sister urged me to send it to a publisher. I bought a copy of *Writer's Market* to figure out how to do that. I learned I needed an agent first, so I sent the manuscript to one. It was immediately rejected. I know traditionally published authors tell of submitting a manuscript to dozens of agents or publishers before getting a nibble. But for me, once was enough."

"You didn't like rejection?"

"It wasn't the rejection, it was the process. I hated

it. Seriously. So instead of sending it to another agent, I filed the book away, and wrote my second historical romance. And then my third."

Brady couldn't help but laugh. The image of her writing books without looking for a publisher somehow appealed to him. She was writing for the love of writing, and he respected her for that.

"So what happened, Ella?"

"I stumbled across a blog about self-publishing. I started looking for other online articles and blogs, and eventually signed up for a free publishing account at Amazon. I decided I wanted to do it right, so I asked several of my friends to beta read for me."

"Beta read? What's that?"

"Oh, they read the manuscript and give me honest feedback. From there I did some re-writing, and then I hired a professional editor to edit the manuscript, and my sister, who is an artist, designed my book cover. I'm pretty computer savvy, so creating a file to upload at Amazon wasn't too difficult. I immediately started getting my other manuscripts ready for publication, in much the same way as the first, and my sales really took off after I had five books online, which I did within six months. Of course, it helped that I had already written them."

"That's interesting. So you just publish eBooks at Amazon?"

"No. I also publish at other sites, like Barnes and Noble and Smashwords. My books are also available in paperback, and sold online. But I don't sell many of those."

"Impressive, you get to make a living doing what you love without the burden of notoriety."

"Yeah, I suppose so. I guess it really isn't possible to become a successful musician and still maintain your privacy."

"I suppose I could have made a decent living being a musician and still maintained my privacy, to some degree."

"Ah, but you would not be a star." Ella was careful to say star, and not rock star.

"No, I would not be a star. And for as much as I hate the loss of my privacy, I love what I do. I really do." Brady realized in that moment that a few days earlier he might not have expressed that sentiment. But it was true; he loved his career.

"Have you always been into music?" Ella asked.

"My dad was a musician; I suppose it started with him."

"What does he think of your success?"

Before answering the question, Brady wondered how much she'd read about his past, when she initially looked him up online. She obviously didn't know his father, like his mother, was deceased.

"My father died when I was in fourth grade."

"Oh, I'm so sorry. I didn't know. That must have been rough. Did your mother remarry?"

"Actually, my parents were never married. Mom

met my father when he was playing some local dive. They had an affair and she got pregnant. I guess you could say she was a groupie. I don't think for a moment it was a monogamous relationship for him."

"Was your father someone I might have heard about?"

"Considering you didn't know who I was, no." Brady chuckled. "But no, probably not, even if you were more attuned to the music world. According to my mother, he was very talented, but he did what many in my world do: drugs. Lots of drugs. He died of an overdose."

"Oh, I'm sorry, Brady." Ella's sentiments were sincere. "Was he in your life at all?"

"Yeah, actually he was. I'd see him about once a week. My mother was crazy about him, and I assume they were still having sex, now that I look back on that time from an adult's perspective. He never lived with us, but he would stay over sometimes. He taught me how to play the guitar. When he died, that is the only thing of his I got. And I suspect the only reason I got it is that he happened to leave it at our house but died before he could pick it up."

"Your mother never married?"

"No, and she was estranged from her parents. Like me, she was an only child. I think I met my grandparents once, and they died when I was in high school. Mom had her own issues with substance abuse. She worked as a waitress most of her life, and we moved around a lot. She died a few months after I turned eighteen. I already had a band, and was working at local dives. I suppose the one thing my parents taught me—stay away from drugs."

"I'm sorry, Brady."

"It all worked out for me. I wish my mother had lived to see my success. I would have liked to have made her life easier."

"Was it the drugs?" Ella asked in a soft voice.

"You mean, what killed her?"

She replied with a nod.

"No, she had breast cancer. Unfortunately, she never took very good care of herself, and never went to the doctor, unless it was an absolute emergency. By the time she finally went, it was too advanced, and she went fairly quick. So, what about your family?"

"Mine?" Ella felt uncomfortable, since hers seemed like the ideal family, compared to his.

"Well, I have an older sister, Connie, the artist. We're pretty close, I guess. But she moved to California last year with her husband, so we pretty much keep in touch with Facetime. My father was in the insurance business. Nothing too exciting, but he made a good living. Mom was a nurse. They both retired about a year ago, and have been doing the RV thing. I'm the only one in our family who still lives in our hometown. They all left home but me!"

"You said this cabin belonged to your parents once?"

"Yeah, it belonged to my family. I've been coming up here for as long as I can remember. When my parents retired last year, they talked of selling the cabin and I about freaked out. I just couldn't bear the thought of losing it. I realized it wasn't really fair to expect them to keep it, considering they'd been dreaming of traveling after they retired, and maintaining a cabin really didn't fit neatly into the picture. So I bought it."

"Sounds like you have a little problem with change," he gently teased.

"Hmm, you noticed that? I pitched a total fit when my sister moved to California. Her husband got this killer job offer, and of course, they were going to move. But I do hate change. Unfortunately, the world is constantly changing, and there doesn't seem to be anything I can do about it."

"Do your parents know you're up here? You think they're worried about you?"

"I told them I was coming up. They aren't in the habit of checking up on me when I'm at the cabin, and the phone going out is not that unusual. They're on their way to California to spend Thanksgiving with Connie. I was invited along, but I had this book to finish. Mom didn't understand why I couldn't go too, since I work at home. *You can write anywhere,* she told me."

"But you can't." Brady chuckled.

"No, I can't. I can't write with people around. By

the way, I really appreciate the fact you don't bug me when I'm writing."

"Don't bug you?" He laughed at her choice of words.

"The last time I came up here I planned to write, and Craig insisted on joining me. But when we got here, whenever I tried to get some writing done, he would wander in the room after fifteen minutes and ask me what I was writing, or if I wanted something to eat, or tell me he wanted me to play hooky from the writing and go for a walk. While I understand the concept of taking time out to smell the flowers, when it's time to work, I need to write."

"I completely understand. Which reminds me; I've been having difficulty with lyrics on a new song. Would you mind listening to it, and telling me what you think? Maybe you can offer a fresh perspective."

"Remember, I'm not really a rock and roll person," Ella warned, a little self-conscious.

"Please, this one really isn't hard rock. I'd love to know what you think."

Ella and Brady spent the next hour in the down-stairs bedroom, sitting on the bed as Brady ran through the song he had been working on. Ella was surprised to discover she didn't hate it, and was able to offer him sound advice.

When they realized it was past midnight, Ella announced it was time for her to go to bed. They both stood up, and Brady walked her to the bedroom doorway.

"I really appreciate your help. You had a great suggestion," Brady told her, sincere in his praise. They stood silently for a moment in the doorway, Ella leaning back casually on the doorjamb, while Brady leaned against his right hand, which he propped against the wall above her head.

Ella smiled up at Brady, feeling mellow from the wine and enjoying the feeling of camaraderie she'd shared with him all evening. Something twisted in her stomach when she looked into his blue eyes and noted the intent way he was looking at her.

Before she had time to say goodnight and slip from the room, Brady leaned toward her and brushed his lips over hers, ever so lightly. When he pulled away, it was obvious by his expression the kiss surprised him as much as it did her. Immediately, he dropped his right hand to his side and stood up straight. Ella also straightened her posture, her eyes wide in surprise.

"Why did you do that?" Ella asked, sincere in her question.

"I guess," Brady answered after a moment of silence, his voice barely a whisper, "I've been wanting to kiss you for sometime." Without another word, Ella turned and dashed into the hallway, escaping to her bedroom on the second floor.

CHAPTER THIRTEEN

It wasn't until they were sitting at the breakfast bar the next morning, side-by-side and eating scrambled eggs and bacon that Ella brought up the kiss.

"Brady, about that kiss," she began.

"It wasn't much of a kiss," Brady told her as he angrily chomped down on a piece of crisp bacon, jerking the bottom end from his mouth as if he were eating beef jerky. "Hardly worth discussing."

"Then I take it you won't be kissing me again."

"I don't know. Do you want me to kiss you again?" Brady turned to look at her as he asked the question. He seemed annoyed and somewhat edgy.

"It probably isn't a good idea," Ella told him, refusing to meet his gaze.

"Probably? Why not? Didn't you like it? I couldn't tell. When you ran from the room, I wasn't sure if you liked the kiss but were afraid, or hated kissing me and needed to get upstairs to wash your mouth out with Listerine."

"It wasn't a matter of liking the kiss, but what is the point?"

"Perhaps I should kiss you again, but this time put a little more effort into it so we can have a better discussion," Brady snapped.

"Why are you so grouchy this morning?" Ella's eyes filled with tears. She hoped to have a serious discussion with him, but his attitude unnerved her.

"Oh fuck," Brady said under his breath, when he noticed tears glistening in her expressive blue-green eyes. "Please don't cry."

"I'm not crying!" she insisted.

"Why do women always want to talk about this kind of stuff?"

"Then tell me Brady, what do you want to do?"

"For starters..." Brady turned in the barstool to face her. He grabbed hold of her right arm and forced her to face him. "I would like to kiss you again, and then I would like to take your clothes off. The only thing I regret about that damn kiss is not doing it better, and letting you leave."

"Brady, I'm not one of your adoring fans who'll eagerly jump at the chance to get into your bed."

"You don't think I know that? If you were, I wouldn't want you."

"Is that what this is about?" Ella asked, jerking her arm from his grasp. "Just a challenge?"

"That is not what I meant," Brady said, angry with himself for his choice of words. Restlessly he combed his right hand through his hair and got up from the barstool. He began to pace back and forth, next to the breakfast bar.

"No, Ella, this is not about some challenge or ego conquest. I-I'm crazily attracted to you. I have been for days."

"Brady, casual sex is not really my thing. I confess I find you attractive. I guess I'm really no different from the other women. I find you very sexy. But I'm sorry, that isn't enough for me."

"What are you saying?"

"Brady, when I get involved sexually with a man, it's because we are starting a relationship. It doesn't necessarily mean it will be forever, or that it'll last, but it means we are both committed to trying to see where the relationship takes us. I don't see that for us." Ella sounded sad when she spoke the words.

"I'm not asking for a one night stand, Ella. I like you, very much."

"I like you too, Brady," Ella said in a soft voice. Getting off the barstool, she stood before him and took one of his hands in hers.

"I'm not a fool. When the roads are clear again, you'll head back to your life and I'll return to mine.

That will be much easier to do if we don't complicate our friendship with sex. I'm afraid I'm not great with casual sex."

"What I feel about you isn't casual," Brady insisted.

"And what happens when we go home, then what?"

"I don't know; do we have to think about that now?" He pulled his hand from her grasp and began pacing again.

"Brady, we've only known each other for a little over a week."

"Considering we've spent hours together, eaten every meal together, I figure that is at least twenty dates. Don't you normally have sex by the twentieth date?"

"Only if I think there is a future in the relationship. And frankly, I can't see beyond the snowstorm."

Without saying another word, Ella picked up the plates from the breakfast bar and set them in the sink. Instead of washing the dishes, she went upstairs to write. Brady stood by the staircase for a moment. He heard her enter the spare bedroom upstairs and shut the door behind her.

After a moment, he turned and walked to the kitchen sink and started washing the breakfast dishes. He thought about what Ella said, and began feeling guilty over his words. It had been years since a woman had told him *no*. Now, he found it immensely frustrating that the one woman he desired wasn't interested in what he had to offer. *But what was he offering*? He asked himself.

Brady glanced outside. By the looks of the snow, he didn't imagine he would be leaving within the next few days. It was foolish, he told himself, to make their time uncomfortable, especially when he sincerely liked her.

He finished the dishes, then went to his bedroom and grabbed a pad of paper he'd been using earlier. Tearing several blank sheets of paper from the pad, he took them and an ink pen to the breakfast bar, sat down, and began writing a letter.

When he was done, Brady reread the letter before folding it neatly in two. On the blank side of the paper, he wrote *Ella*.

Making his way quickly up the stairs, he shoved the folded note under the door to the spare bedroom, knocked once on the door, and then turned and headed back downstairs.

Ella was sitting at her desk, staring blankly at the computer screen when she heard the knock at the door. Turning from the computer, she saw the note on the floor, shoved halfway into the room.

A few moments later, she stood quietly, alone in the small room, reading Brady's words.

Dear Ella, I guess I was an ass again. It is a bad habit

of mine. I'm sorry I made you uncomfortable and even sorrier for my careless words. You have been nothing but kind to me, and you don't deserve my attitude.

I consider you a friend, and I hope you consider me one. If it wasn't for you, I would probably be buried several feet under the snow. Yet, it isn't just the fact you came to my rescue, opened your home to me, fed me—you have also helped me regain something of my former self.

I forgot what it felt like to be friends with someone who didn't expect something from me, who wasn't more charmed by my fame than the person I am inside.

Because I consider you a friend, I'll be honest with you. I can't remember when I've been so attracted to a woman—like I am with you. I'd be quite content to spend the next week in bed with you. It's not because you're playing hard to get. For one thing, I have long since learned you don't play games. That is one thing I love about you.

But you are also right to question what happens next —after the snowstorm, when we return to reality. You and I lead such different lives. I'm in no position to suggest there will be something for us when we leave the mountain. But it isn't because I don't want you in my life. It's because I understand how drastically your life would change if you became part of mine.

I promise to keep my hands and lips to myself for the rest of my stay with you. And I hope you will accept my apology and allow us to go back to where we were yesterday, before I kissed you.

But if you decide you would like that second kiss, it will be your call. Brady."

A smile formed on her lips and several tears escaped and slid down her face. She wiped them away with the back of her hand.

A few minutes before noon, Ella came downstairs with Sam close on her heels. On her way to take Sam outside, she popped her head in the bedroom doorway, where Brady was working on his music. She found him sitting on his bed, his attention focused on the iPad.

"Hungry?" Ella asked cheerfully.

"Is it lunchtime already?"

"Almost. I'm going to take Sam out first. How does tuna fish sound?"

"Works for me. Let me wrap this up; I'll be just a few minutes."

"No hurry," Ella told him.

Thirty minutes later, Ella was sitting on the couch, taking her last bite of the tuna fish sandwich when she said, "I got an idea when I took Sam outside."

"What's that?" He sat on the recliner next to the couch eating the last of the potato chips on his plate. He'd wolfed down the sandwich minutes earlier.

"It's almost Thanksgiving. When I was a kid, we used to come up here every year at this time. One thing we always did that week… we'd put lights on the small pine tree out back. I think we should decorate the tree. I saw the lights in the attic."

"Is it safe putting lights up in the snow?" Brady asked.

"Well, we won't plug them in until the tree is decorated and they are outdoor lights. I don't see a problem. We used to do it every year."

"Aren't those lights kind of old? I'd hate to burn down your cabin."

"No, silly." Ella laughed. "The lights in the attic are only a couple years old. Dad replaced them several years ago. They should be fine."

"Well, sure, I'm game. Hell, I haven't decorated a Christmas tree in years."

"Are you serious?"

"I've been living in a hotel, remember? But it sounds like fun."

"Then let's do it! It's not snowing now." Ella jumped up from the couch. "I'm going upstairs to change into some warmer clothes."

"Okay, I'll do the same. I'll meet you in the garage to get our boots and gloves."

Ella flashed Brady a smile and she raced up the stairs. Sam trotted after her. Brady leaned back in the recliner for a moment. Closing his eyes, he smiled to himself, grateful that Ella appeared to have accepted his apology and they were back to where they were the day before.

Before he could go change his clothes, Ella called down to him.

"Brady, can you help me get the stuff from the attic?"

"Okay, I can't let those attic people get you!" he shouted up to her, as he sprinted up the stairs to the second floor.

In the attic, Ella knew exactly where to find the Christmas lights. The extension cords were in another box and she placed it atop the box of lights, before handing it to Brady to carry downstairs. He could barely see over the boxes.

"I usually get minions to do this kind of stuff for me," Brady grumbled as he made his way down the stairs, careful not to trip. Ella laughed at his mock outrage. Once downstairs, he set the box in the garage before going back to his room to change clothes.

"How are we supposed to put lights on that?" Brady asked, noting the snow-laden branches of the small pine tree. They stood together in the backyard. The box of lights sat in the snow nearby and Sam leapt around the backyard, leaving paw tracks in the snow.

"First we do this," Ella explained. She stepped closer to the tree, reached in the branches with one of her gloved hands and grabbed the center of the pine tree. Giving it a vigorous shake, the snow fell from the tree's limbs, much of it landing atop Brady. He let out a little whopping sound and jumped backwards. In his attempt to move out of the way, he tripped over Sam before landing on his buttock in the snow.

"Stop fooling around," Ella teased. "You can make snow angels later."

"You could have warned me you were going to do that!" Brady told her as he got up from the snow, stumbling a few times before he was able to stand erect.

"Well, gee, what fun is that?" Ella asked with a giggle.

After brushing the snow off his clothes, Brady took one strand of lights from the box. They were fairly tangled.

"I guess we should have done that part in the garage," Ella told him, annoyed with herself for not thinking of that before coming out in the snow.

"Yeah, I haven't hung Christmas lights since I was in high school. Now that I think about it, I believe we missed the step where we untangle the lights and check the bulbs." Without saying another word, Brady picked up the box with the lights and cords and headed back to the garage.

It was an hour later before the strands were untangled and the faulty bulbs replaced. It took another hour to string the lights around the tree. Brady held onto one end while Ella walked around the small pine tree holding the strand of lights, strate-gically placing it on the branches.

It was late in the afternoon and the sky was getting dark with clouds when they were finally done. Much to their delight, the lights turned on the first time they were plugged in. Ella explained the electrical outlet was connected to a switch inside the cabin, so they would be able to turn the lights on and off from inside.

They were getting cold, so they raced back to the cabin with Brady carrying the now empty box. In the garage, they removed their shoes, gloves and coats. Ella offered to make some hot chocolate, which suddenly sounded better than hot tea or wine. Brady offered to stoke the fire while she prepared the hot beverage.

Ella topped the two mugs of hot chocolate with a liberal dollop of sweet whipped cream and carried the mugs over to Brady, who now stood at the side window admiring the tree.

"We do good work," he told her as he accepted the steaming mug.

"Yes we do. It looks pretty, doesn't it? Especially with the snow. I like the way the colors glisten off it."

"It doesn't look like the other pine trees in the area."

"It isn't. Dad planted it one year. It was one of those live Christmas trees."

"This was fun. Thanks Ella." Brady couldn't remember the last time he had been so content.

"You're welcome. It *was* fun. Thanks for helping me, Brady. I couldn't have done it alone."

"Yeah, there're some things that are more fun to do with someone else." His voice was barely audible.

CHAPTER FOURTEEN

Ella didn't return to her manuscript until late that afternoon. When dinner hour rolled around, she felt it necessary to keep writing, so she called down to Brady, telling him she would be skipping dinner and to go ahead and fix something for himself when he was hungry. Several hours passed and she heard a knock. A little irritated at being disturbed, she got up from the desk and opened the door. Ella was surprised to see no one was there, but when she looked down at the floor, she noticed the plate of food Brady had left for her, along with a note.

The note read: *You need to keep up your strength. See you in the morning. Thanks again for this afternoon.*

Touched by the thoughtful gesture, Ella felt guilty for her initial annoyance when hearing the knock.

She picked up the plate and took it with her to the desk.

The next morning Ella slept late, waking up a few minutes past 10:00 a.m. The first thing she noticed when she woke up was the sunshine. Rolling out of bed, she sleepily made her way to the bedroom window. There was not a single cloud in the clear blue sky. Already the bright sun was melting the snow in the yard below.

She'd skipped her bath the night before, so she showered and washed her hair. The moment she stepped out of the shower, she smelled the coffee brewing. Anxious to get downstairs she roughly towel dried her hair and hastily pulled a comb through it to remove the tangles. Instead of getting dressed, she threw on her floor length robe and headed to the kitchen.

"Good morning, sleepy head," Brady greeted when she came downstairs. He'd already poured her a cup of coffee, and he handed it to her the minute she got to the foot of the staircase. Wearing a clean white T-shirt, grey sweatpants and white socks, he flashed Ella a welcoming smile. His dark hair was damp and combed back. Apparently, he too had recently showered.

"I slept late," she stated the obvious and accepted the coffee. "This smells wonderful, thanks."

"I figured you needed your sleep. You stayed up past 2 a.m." Brady's eyes swept over Ella's robe clad body. Instead of buttons securing the front of the garment, she had tied a blue fabric belt loosely around her waist.

"How did you know that?" Ella asked as she moved to the living room window and looked outside.

"I heard you go back to your room after two," Brady explained, standing beside her.

"I'm sorry, did I wake you up?" she asked apologetically.

"No, I couldn't sleep myself. In fact, I just woke up about thirty minutes ago."

"It looks like it's going to be a beautiful day today," Ella told him, taking another sip of the coffee.

"It certainly does," Brady agreed.

Then they heard it, the snowplow, moving slowly and steadily up the street, clearing the road.

Sadness washed over Ella and she felt a twisting sensation in the pit of her stomach. She didn't want this time to end. Unable to contain the unexpected emotion, tears filled her eyes. Standing still, afraid to look over at Brady, she bit down on her lower lip, determined not to cry. Unable to suppress the tears, they slid silently down her face.

Brady stood beside Ella, battling his own conflicting emotions when he glanced over at her and noticed the tears.

"Ella, what's wrong?" He took the coffee cup from her trembling hands and set it with his on the windowsill, and then he took hold of her shoulders, turning her to face him. The moment he asked the question, he intuitively knew the answer.

"I don't want this to end," Ella blurted out, her blue-green eyes sparkling with unshed tears.

Without thought or consideration, Ella reached up and took hold of Brady's face, pulling his lips to hers. He did not resist. Wrapping his arms around her, Brady pulled her close, fully participating in the shared intimacy. Their lips parted and his tongue slipped into her moist mouth. She accepted the intrusion and wrapped her arms around his neck. Their bodies pressed together as the kiss deepened and hearts raced.

A sense of urgency washed over Brady. His hands moved from Ella's waist and slid in the front of her robe, pushing aside the unwanted fabric belt strap. With minimal effort, it untied, and the front of her robe opened, giving Brady full access to Ella's nude body.

Ella let out a little gasp when she felt his hands move over the bare skin of her waist and hips, but she did not resist. He pulled her away from the window, toward his bedroom. Refusing to end the kiss, they stumbled awkwardly along the way, the kiss frantic, Ella losing her robe in the hallway. Anxiously she tugged on his T-shirt. They broke the kiss for just a moment, enabling Ella to jerk the T-shirt off, up over Brady's head as they entered the downstairs bedroom.

Once they stumbled into the bedroom, Brady pushed Ella onto the bed, sending her sprawling across the mattress, fully nude and unashamed. Eagerly, he looked down at her. Standing beside the bed he hastily removed the sweatpants as Ella watched.

Her eyes glistened, this time not from tears but from passion. Brady smiled down at her and noted the way she moistened her lips in anticipation of what was to come. Kicking off his socks, and fully nude, Brady moved onto the bed, covering Ella. The kissing resumed and Ella wrapped her legs around Brady's waist, welcoming him inside without hesitation or thought.

Thirty minutes later, the two lovers lay sprawled on the mattress, each staring up at the ceiling, trying to steady their labored breaths. Content smiles played on each pair of lips, and while Ella looked slightly dazed, Brady looked smugly satisfied.

"We've sure been wasting a lot of time," Brady said at last. Ella murmured something, and while her exact words were discernible, he was fairly certain she agreed with his statement. Ella rolled over toward him, and with a quick motion climbed atop his nude body. Straddling his hips, she leaned over him, her hands resting on his shoulders.

"This probably isn't the best time to mention

this," Brady said, running his hands up each side of her slim body. "We didn't have protected sex."

Ella sighed then said, "Well, I'm on the pill." Instead of dwelling on the fact they failed to use a condom, he reached up and pulled her to him for a kiss. They made love again.

Brady and Ella spent the rest of the morning and early afternoon in bed. By the time they left Brady's room and looked outside, the streets were cleared. Neither one checked to see if the phone was working.

Hunger pangs finally set in, and the two went to the kitchen to make something to eat. Ella wore her robe and Brady his sweat pants. It was almost 3:00 p.m.

"You know, you don't have to leave just because the roads are clear," Ella said in a quiet voice as she stood at the kitchen counter making two peanut butter sandwiches. Brady stepped behind her and wrapped his arms around her waist before nibbling on her neck. She squirmed, yet moved her head to one side to give him better access to the tender flesh.

"I was hoping you'd say that," Brady said between nibbles.

"Of course, we should probably do something about your Jeep," Ella said, closing her eyes and enjoying his touch.

"I suppose. But it isn't in anyone's way. We can do that tomorrow; we have other more important things to do."

"Like what?" Ella asked with a giggle.

"For one, make up for all this time we wasted." Brady slipped one hand in the front of her robe and seized a breast, holding it firmly in his grasp. He gave it a gentle squeeze before rubbing his thumb over her nipple.

"Oh!" Ella cried out from sheer pleasure. "And how am I supposed to get any writing done with you constantly molesting me?"

"Not my problem, sexy Ella."

Ella laughed at his naughty behavior and nudged him away with one of her hips before refastening her robe. She picked up one of the peanut butter sandwiches sitting on the counter and shoved it in his mouth.

"Here," she said with mock seriousness. "If you're to keep me satisfied, you need to maintain your strength. I'll not have you fainting from malnutrition."

Brady grabbed the sandwich and tore off a bite before saying, "You are a demanding mistress."

"And just you remember that," Ella scolded before playfully swatting his backside.

"We could drive up later to the cabin I rented and see what interesting food your friend stocked in the pantry."

"Not a bad idea. I suppose we shouldn't let it go to waste."

"About the Jeep. Maybe it would be better if I just

call a tow company and have them get it out of the ditch, charge the battery and deliver it here or at the cabin I rented. There's really no reason for us to go do it."

"Well, I'm not even sure I have battery cables, so that's probably what we'll have to do. Let's see if the phone is working yet." Ella picked up the phone in the kitchen and held the receiver up to her ear. It was dead. "No, still out. But now that the snowplow is clearing the road, I bet the phone will be working in a couple of hours or so."

Agreeing the Jeep could wait, they finished the sandwiches, each had a glass of milk and then took Sam outside to do her business before heading upstairs to try out Ella's bed.

CHAPTER FIFTEEN

"Hey, Susan, get ahold of Amanda over at cabin rentals. We've a Jeep up here that looks like it's been stuck for at least a week." Standing on the side of the road, the sheriff leaned against his vehicle as he spoke into the radio's microphone.

"According to the registration the owner is a Kevin Jones. See if he's one of hers. Find out if he's accounted for. We also found a cell phone, down the road from the Jeep, one of those fancy ones. Battery's dead. Not sure if it belongs to the Jeep, but it doesn't look good."

Almost an hour later, Amanda reached her cousin by phone. She had been frantically calling his cell phone and leaving messages at his hotel. While she tried to contact him, her husband, Chad drove up to the mountains to check out the nearby cabins. He had just returned, and was standing by her desk when she finally reached Kevin.

"Have you heard from Brady in the last few days?" She fidgeted nervously as she asked.

"What are you talking about Amanda? The last time we spoke you told me not to expect a call from him because the phones were out and there's no cell service on the mountain."

"The phones have been working up there for at least ten hours. And, Kevin, they found your Jeep on the side of the road. It looks like it's been stuck there since the blizzard hit."

"What about Brady?" Kevin shouted into the phone.

"We haven't found him. Chad drove up there. He wasn't at the rental, but that didn't surprise me because it's a good distance from where they found the Jeep. They also found a cell phone, and they're fairly certain it belongs to Brady, but you will need to look at it to be sure because the battery's dead."

"Maybe he's holed up at one of the other cabins," Kevin suggested.

"Chad checked all the cabins in the area. They're still locked up. My friend Ella Lewis is the only one up there right now, but her cabin is some distance from where they found the Jeep. If he was with Ella, she would've called me by now."

"Can you at least check with her?"

"I've tried calling her but I think she unplugged

her phone. That doesn't surprise me because she's a writer, and she went up there for the isolation. Ella doesn't even have Internet or cable, because she says it is too much of a distraction. Chad stopped by her cabin when he was up there. Her Suburban was in the garage and there was a fire burning in her fireplace. He knocked on the door and heard her dog bark, but she didn't answer. She was probably upstairs writing and didn't hear him. He peeked in the front window and didn't see anything unusual or to indicate Brady was there. But I'll definitely keep trying to call her. If I can't get her on the phone, I'll drive up there with Chad.

"But, Kevin, there are a number of other cabins he would have come across before reaching Ella's. Plus, she's one of my oldest friends. I know she would have called me by now if he somehow ended up at her place."

"I'm coming," Kevin announced. "Talk to the sheriff and see if they can keep this thing under wraps. The last thing we need is a hoard of TV people descending on Shipley. And I doubt your sheriff would be too thrilled having them get in the way."

"Kevin, it will take you hours to get here."

"I'm not going to drive. I know where I can rent a plane. The pilot's a good friend of Brady's. Is the airstrip clear?"

"Chad," Amanda covered the mouthpiece of her

phone for a moment and directed her conversation to her husband, who stood quietly listening. "Have they plowed the airstrip? Kevin wants to fly in."

"I don't think so, but I'll get Fred to do it. He wasn't that far from here." Not waiting for Amanda to reply, he dashed from the office to find the snow-plow driver.

"Chad's going to handle it, Kevin. Fly safe."

It is not easy to keep a secret in a small mountain village, especially when a famous celebrity has been reported missing—lost in a blizzard for over one week. Kevin managed to make it to Shipley within two hours after Amanda contacted him. He arrived in a rented Cessna, which landed on a freshly plowed dirt airstrip at the foot of the mountain.

As they approached for the landing, Kevin looked out the plane and let out a curse.

"I guess they didn't keep it quiet," the pilot observed. "I sure as hell hope we find Brady safe and sound in some cabin, and we can all laugh about this someday."

"I hope you're right, Nick."

Amanda and Chad waited alongside the dirt airstrip and watched as Nick easily landed the Cessna. After Kevin introduced Nick to his cousin and her husband, he and Chad helped tie down the plane. The four squeezed into the front cab of the pickup and drove into the village, which was only a few minutes away.

"I'm sorry, Kevin," Amanda told him as they drove down Main Street toward the Sheriff's office. Parked vehicles were everywhere and people swarmed the street, many carrying cameras.

When they pulled up at the sheriff's office, news people greeted them, rudely shouting questions at Kevin, while shoving microphones in his face. Amanda and Chad silently ushered Kevin and the pilot into the sheriff's office, ignoring the questions.

Once in the office, with the news people outside, the sheriff explained they were arranging a search. Minutes later, Kevin was shown the cell phone, and he confirmed it belonged to the missing rock star.

UP ON THE MOUNTAIN, AT ELLA'S CABIN, THE TWO lovers had no idea what was brewing in the small village. Earlier, Ella had heard someone knock on her door, followed by Sam's bark. When she finally looked out the window, she spied Chad's truck drive away. Not ready to leave the private cocoon she and Brady had created, Ella had made no attempt to stop the truck.

It was on their second day as lovers when the landline began to ring. Instead of answering the call, Ella impulsively unplugged the phone and tossed it in a drawer. Brady only laughed, and made love to her again.

The two eventually wandered back downstairs, knowing they couldn't ignore Sam forever. She needed to be taken outside. After that task was accomplished, they went into the downstairs bedroom.

The window faced the back yard and not the street, so they left the blinds open, still assuming they were virtually alone on the mountain. Never once did they consider someone might find the Jeep and start a search for the driver.

Making love on the bed and facing away from the window, they failed to notice the two strange men walking around the corner of the cabin. Sam rarely barked, even when strangers were outside. Had they knocked on the door, she would have. But the men didn't knock; instead, they made their way around the cabin, peeking in all the windows.

One man, with a camera hanging from his neck, looked in the window of the downstairs bedroom. He paused a moment, not quite believing what he was seeing. There sprawled on the bed, oblivious to the fact there was an audience, was the missing rock star, Brady Gates, energetically screwing a tasty little number.

He raised his camera to the window and began clicking away, digitally capturing the intimate scene. There was no need for a flash, so the photographer was able to take at least twenty images before Ella turned her face in his direction.

She let out a high-pitched scream and practically tossed Brady from her body, before rolling off the bed and out of the men's view. Instead of fleeing, the photographer snapped a few more photographs before making his retreat and racing to the car with his companion. He would have the photographs uploaded to the Internet within the hour.

Brady grabbed his pants and pulled them on while rushing from the bedroom. By the time he got to the living room and looked out the window, the two men were driving away. Unfortunately, theirs was not the only car on the street. One of the men in the car leaned out the window and pointed to the cabin, causing several of the other vehicles to turn around and drive toward Ella's cabin.

Brady immediately shut the blinds and rushed around the cabin locking the doors and closing the window blinds.

"What the hell is going on?" Ella shouted, now standing in the hallway wearing her robe. She combed her fingers through her hair.

"I'm sorry, babe, but I'm afraid our little secret is out," Brady told her as he rushed from window to window.

"Who were those men? Did they take our pictures?"

"I'm afraid so. You better go get dressed, because we can't stay locked up in the cabin." He peered out a window. "Fuck, there's already a half dozen cars parked along the street. People are getting out of them and coming in this direction."

Ella raced up the stairs to her bedroom. She began to cry.

Brady felt sick. He walked back into the down-stairs bedroom, forgetting he hadn't closed the blinds when rushing out to the living room. Several people were standing outside the cabin looking in, shamelessly snapping pictures of the room and its unmade bed. Brady could only imagine the headlines – *Brady Gates's Secret Love Nest.*

Angrily, Brady walked to the window and jerked the blinds closed, ignoring the paparazzi outside and the fact they were eagerly snapping his picture. Grabbing some fresh clothes from his suitcase, he walked to the bathroom and dressed.

Brady found Ella upstairs sitting on the side of her bed, tears streaming down her face. The bedroom lights were off and the blinds closed. He walked to Ella and sat by her side, on the edge of the mattress, wrapping one arm around her.

"I'm truly sorry this happened, Ella. But you need to pull yourself together and wash your face. You don't want them to see you cry."

Irritated with his words, Ella jerked away from his touch. "They aren't going to see me again, so if I feel like crying, I will."

"I'm afraid that isn't the way it works."

"They had no right taking my picture! They trespassed on my property. I'm going to sue their asses!" Anger replaced her tears.

"You can try, Ella, but sometimes it's best just to handle these situations and move on." Brady stood up and paced the room.

"Exactly what do they intend to do with those photographs?" Ella asked.

"They might show up in one of those rags, or on the Internet," Brady answered in a dull voice.

"But I was naked!" Ella screeched.

"Ella, it's time to plug the phone in. I have a feeling you need to call Amanda. Considering the people surrounding the cabin, I think someone's found the Jeep."

"The Jeep?"

"I should have considered that. I imagine they noticed the Jeep when plowing the road. Someone probably connected it to me, which explains all those people swarming around the cabin right now."

Reluctant to let in more of the outside world, Ella refused to plug the phone in. Giving her time to adjust to the new set of circumstances, Brady sat back down on the edge of the mattress and wrapped an arm around Ella, pulling her protectively to his side. She leaned into him and closed her eyes. They sat in silence for about twenty minutes. Finally, Ella took a deep breath and decided to do what Brady suggested.

Wiping the tears from her face with the back of

her hand, Ella removed the phone from the drawer and plugged it in. The moment she did, it began to ring.

"Hello?" Ella said, answering the phone.

"Ella, oh my god, is Brady Gates there?" came the frantic voice.

"Amanda? What in the hell is going on?" Ella sat on the side of the bed and glanced up at Brady, who watched her.

"Is Brady Gates with you?" Amanda asked.

"Yes, what's wrong?"

"Everyone is looking for him! Ella, some photographers just returned to town—they're saying things about you and Brady. They say they have pictures."

Ella groaned and closed her eyes for a moment. She stood up and walked to the window, still holding the phone. Peeking out the window, she was surprised to see the number of cars and people surrounding the cabin.

"Amanda, we need to get Brady off this mountain. There are people everywhere outside. Get the sheriff up here and have them get these jerks off my property."

"My cousin is here. He flew in. We'll come for Brady, and take him to the airstrip. He can fly out within the hour with Kevin and the pilot. I'll talk to Chad and get some help from the other firemen to keep the crowd away from the airstrip. Have him ready to go. We'll be there soon."

Ella hung up the phone and looked up at Brady.

"They're coming to get you. Your bodyguard arranged an airplane; it's already here. You're going home, Brady. I guess you better get your things together. Amanda said they'll be here soon."

CHAPTER SIXTEEN

"At least they're staying off your property," Amanda commented. She stood at the living room window of Ella's cabin looking outside. It was a sunny November day, and most of the snow had already melted. Ella was in the kitchen area preparing a pot of green tea to share with her friend. The two women were alone in the cabin.

"True, but taking Sam outside has become a major pain in the ass. At least they leave at night. Where are they staying anyway?"

"At the RV park in the village."

"I wondered if they were renting some of your cabins."

"No. A few called, but I told them the cabins were closed up for the winter."

"You think some of your owners will be upset

with you, passing up this opportunity? I imagine some are willing to pay well, especially for the cabins close to here."

"It wasn't a difficult call, Ella. Considering the lack of respect they showed to you, I can't imagine they would treat a rental cabin with respect."

"Well, I would have thought they'd be bored with me by now, and move on."

"It's only been a couple days." Amanda turned from the window, walked to the recliner, and sat down. Her baby bump was more prominent than the last time Ella and she met at the rental office.

"Here, it's hot, so be careful." Ella set a cup of tea on the oak end table next to the recliner.

"Thanks. And you know, Ella," Amanda picked up the cup and gently blew on the hot liquid. "We are talking Brady Gates—the *Brady Gates*. You do realize you're the hot topic of conversation on all the morning talk shows. Not to mention what they're saying late night."

"I know; my sister called me. Wanted to know what the hell was going on. And those pictures...." Ella grimaced. Picking her cup of tea off the breakfast bar she walked to the couch and sat down.

"I still can't believe those guys can get away with that. But Ella, I have to say, you looked good."

"Crap, Amanda, you saw them?"

"I figured as your friend, I should look and let

you know what to expect when you leave this place and get back to the real world. Without television or the Internet, you have no idea what they're saying about you."

"I prefer it that way."

"You can't be an ostrich forever. Anyway, I wouldn't really call the pictures pornographic—just suggestive. You can tell what you two are doing, but honestly, you reveal more in a bikini. Lucky for you, Brady was covering the important parts. He has a very nice butt, by the way."

Ella responded with a snort and took another sip of tea.

"So, what did you tell your sister?"

"Pretty much the same things I told you."

"She didn't get the juicy parts, either?"

"The juicy parts are none of your business. I just wish I could convince those jerks out there it's none of their business, either."

"Have you heard from Brady?"

"No. And I don't expect to. We both knew this wasn't about a relationship. Hopefully, the press and paparazzi will find another story to chase and leave me alone."

"According to the weather report, another storm is moving in. They think it'll be bigger than the last one. That might solve your problem. No way those folks can camp out there in a blizzard."

"Crap, when is it to hit?"

"I heard the day after Thanksgiving."

"I need to make plans to get out of here before then. But I'm not sure where to go."

"Not up to another blizzard?"

"It isn't the blizzard per se. But do you think talk of a storm will scare those people away? Someone is bound to stick it out, and you know what that means?"

"What?"

"Some idiots won't leave and I'll be forced to let them take refuge in my cabin, or risk them freezing to death. While I might prefer to let them freeze, I wouldn't do that. But I certainly don't want to be snowbound with them!"

"You have a point. Plus, I wouldn't be surprised if some would welcome a storm, knowing you would have to let them into your cabin. So, where will you go, home or your sister's in California?"

"Both places are out of the question at this time. I called one of my neighbors, and she tells me reporters have been bothering everyone in the condo complex, trying to dig up dirt on me. From what I understand, they've even tracked down the hair salon I use and several of the businesses I frequent."

"They've been doing that in the village, but I didn't think they'd descend on your condo, especially since you're here. What's wrong with your sister's place?"

"Reporters have been knocking on her door and showing up at her work."

"That's crazy."

"I figure, if I can just hide out for a while, in a few weeks, I'll be yesterday's news and I can get back to my normal life." At that moment, the phone in the kitchen began to ring. Ella set her cup on the coffee table and walked to the kitchen. She looked at the phone, yet didn't pick up the receiver. Letting it ring she returned to the couch and sat down."

"Aren't you going to answer it?" Amanda asked.

"Nope. Thank God for caller ID. I started getting calls from reporters and pranksters right away, so I've been screening my calls. If I don't recognize the number, I don't pick up."

They were quiet for a few minutes, each lost in thought.

"Hey, I know where you can go!" Amanda excitedly suggested. "My brother's house at Morro Bay."

"California?"

"Yeah, not far from San Luis Obispo. His house is about a block from the beach. Nothing fancy, but comfortable. It's a small three bedroom."

"Are they still in Europe?"

"Yeah. The last time I spoke to him he said he's supposed to be transferred back late spring."

"He hasn't rented the house out? I can't imagine leaving it empty."

"No, he refuses to rent it. I have a cousin, in fact

it's Kevin's sister, who takes care of it. She lives over in Cayucos, not too far from his house. She regularly goes over there, moves his vehicle from the garage to the driveway, opens and shuts blinds. Basically, he wants to keep up the appearance that someone lives there. He never got cozy with the neighbors, and most aren't full timers anyway, so I doubt they know the difference."

"If you don't think he would mind, that would be great."

"Sure, I'll call him when I get home. So, how do you plan to get out of here?"

"I know this sounds paranoid, but I thought of it when we were talking about the phone a few minutes ago. I understand law enforcement has the ability to track cell phones. If you can believe those cop shows. I've got an iPhone and I have no idea if some obsessive paparazzi could find a way to track me. I'd like to get one of those throw away phones and leave my iPhone somewhere for a while."

"Considering what you've been through in the last few days, I understand."

"Of course, there's no way for me to get another phone without being seen and I imagine my big ol' Suburban will be easy to track anyway."

The two women sat in silence for a few more minutes, considering the options.

"I've an idea. Chad's driving into Canyon City in

the morning, and he's planning to stop at Walmart. I'll have him pick up a phone. As for the car, take my Mustang and store the Suburban in our garage. You should be able to avoid the reporters if you leave at night and use the back road to come to our house."

"I can't take your car."

"Why? It just sits in the garage this time of the year anyway. In the winter, I normally use our other car, because it has four-wheel drive. The Mustang's in great shape; Chad just had it serviced. It'll do it good to take a road trip."

"Wow, Amanda. That's very generous of you."

"My renter did cause this mess. And who knows, maybe someday you'll share the juicy details."

They both laughed.

"Of course, you'll need to get out of here before that storm hits. At least off the mountain."

"That means I should leave no later than tomorrow night. The next day is Thanksgiving."

"Make sure to leave some lights on, no reason to let them know you're gone. Chad can come up here and close things up for you."

"I'll leave the Christmas tree lights on."

Amanda and Ella chatted for another hour before the two old friends said goodbye and Amanda headed back down to the village. Plotting her escape, Ella started doing her laundry, and cleaning up the cabin.

The next morning, Amanda called and assured Ella everything was a go. Amanda's brother said Ella was welcome to stay in the beach house for as long as needed, provided she was gone when he returned to the States. Chad agreed to pick up a disposable phone, and had already filled up the Mustang's gas tank and checked the oil. The car was ready for a road trip.

Ella kept the blinds on the garage window closed, so a nosy reporter or pushy paparazzi couldn't peek in the window and see she was packing the Suburban. There was still some food left, which she packed in her ice chest. What wouldn't fit in the Mustang, she would leave at Amanda's.

"Will you be spending Thanksgiving alone?" A reporter called out when Ella took Sam outside late that afternoon.

Ella ignored the question, as she had all the others, and went back into the cabin when Sam was finished.

***

"I HAVE TO GIVE YOUR ELLA CREDIT; SHE'S KEEPING HER cool, according to everything I've read," Kevin commented as he surfed the Internet on his iPad, looking for articles on Brady's recent mishap. He sat with his boss on the balcony of Brady's hotel suite.

"She's not my Ella," Brady snapped, taking a quick swig of beer.

"The way you've been stressing over her since you got home, she's obviously something to you."

"This is not home," Brady muttered. Living in a luxury hotel no longer appealed to him.

"Whoa, I wonder how she's going to handle this," Kevin asked, staring at the iPad. He let out a low whistle.

"Handle what?" Brady sat up a little straighter, worried about Ella and the damage he caused.

"According to this article, one of her books is number one over on Amazon, and most of her other books are on the top ten list. Looks like they are also doing well at the other sites. Hmmm, according to this article, all of her books have soared in the charts. Apparently, she's gone from selling just under a hundred books a day to over ten thousand. No reason to worry about Ella. You've propelled her to rock star status in her own field."

Brady reached over and snatched the iPad from Kevin.

"One thing I know about Ella, if her books are selling because she slept with me, that is not going to make her happy." Silently, Brady surfed through the Internet, looking for reviews on Ella's books.

When he found what he was looking for, he quietly read while Kevin watched. After a few minutes a smile formed on Brady's lips, and he began to chuckle.

"What is it?" Kevin asked.

"According to these reviews, curiosity over our relationship may have gotten people to buy her books, but the readers, the reviewers, they love them. In fact, I know one of these reviewers. He absolutely hates my guts, but he loves my Ella."

CHAPTER SEVENTEEN

It was late afternoon when she finally reached Morro Bay. Kevin's sister was there to greet her and show her around the house. After unpacking the Mustang, Ella went to bed, since she had been driving for hours. In spite of her exhaustion, she was unable to fall asleep. Resigned to the fact it was impossible for her to sleep during daylight, she got up and made herself a cup of hot green tea, and headed outside with her laptop, Sam trailing behind her.

Ella sat on a patio chair, her closed laptop propped on her thighs. Breathing deeply, she closed her eyes and drank in the salty fragrance of the ocean. She hadn't been to the coast for several years, and forgot how much she enjoyed it. It wasn't as cold as she expected. Wearing jeans and a pullover sweater kept her warm. Sam sniffed around the courtyard, exploring new scents.

Calm washed over her. There were no paparazzi and intrusive reporters hovering about. She wondered if they were still camped outside her cabin. She'd called her sister to let her know she'd arrived safely, but her phone reception was not terrific, so it was a short call. Ella thought it strange to be in California and not see her sister or parents. Perhaps, when things settled down, she could head south and visit with her family.

Closing her eyes again, she took another deep breath and thought of Brady. She hadn't told anyone —not Amanda or her sister—how much she missed him. Or the fact that she'd fallen in love.

She wondered if he had tried to call her. It was possible, considering she only answered the phone at the cabin when she recognized the number, and she had never known his. While she wanted to think he had tried to call, she seriously doubted that was the case. If he really wanted to contact her, he could have done so through Kevin and Amanda.

With a sigh, she set her cup of tea by her feet on the concrete pavers, opened her laptop and turned it on. She hadn't been online to check her sales reports since leaving Canyon City and heading to the mountains.

Kevin's sister had given her the password to the beach house's wireless Internet connection. In less than five minutes after powering up the laptop, she was online. The first site she opened was Kindle Direct Publishing, to check the sales reports for her eBooks sold at Amazon. She almost dropped the computer from her lap to the patio.

Blinking her eyes in disbelief, she looked closely at the computer screen.

"This has to be some sort of a glitch," she said aloud.

Convinced Amazon had been hacked, she opened the Nook Press site, to check her sales reports at Barnes and Noble. Like the Amazon site, her sales were off the charts.

"This is impossible," she muttered. With disbelief, she opened her Amazon AuthorCentral page and logged into her account. There she could check her author ranking and the ranking of her books published with Amazon. After reading the report, she was stunned. Ella Lewis was a bestselling author.

From Nook Press she went to Goodreads. She was in for another surprise. The last time she checked Goodreads, her best book had been rated less than a hundred times. Now each book had been rated by over 40,000 readers. Her rating average was 4.74 stars, with five stars being the maximum. According to Goodreads, according to her sales stats—readers loved her.

From Goodreads she went to Google search and typed in her pen name. She was astounded by the results. Links to her personal blog, website and books were not the only pages to come up. Her real name and pen name were all over the blogosphere and news sites, and on Twitter, both names were trending.

When the sun began to set, it became too chilly to stay outside, so Ella went back in the beach house. After feeding Sam and making herself a sandwich, she took her laptop with her to the living room and curled up on the couch.

Before resuming her surfing, she opened her email. Once again, she was astounded. Her email box was flooded, and not from the normal spam. There were messages from agents, publishers, media and fans. While a few were unkind and rude, most were supportive.

I think Brady Gates is hot and was curious about his mystery woman. That is the ONLY reason I bought the first book in your Montana series. I admit I expected to hate it. But I loved it! I couldn't put it down! I already started the second one in the series. You rock! Ella received countless emails with similar sentiments.

According to the messages, numerous talk shows wanted her as a guest. Apparently, they had been unable to contact her by phone, and easily located her email on her author's website. It was past midnight when Ella finally turned off the laptop and climbed into bed.

The next morning the ringing of a telephone woke

her. Groggy, Ella reached over to the nightstand and picked up the phone's receiver.

"Happy Thanksgiving, Ella," came her sister's cheerful voice.

"Connie? What time is it?" Ella sat up in bed and rubbed her eyes.

"I don't know, after eight. You still sleeping?"

"Well, I was. Remember, I didn't get any sleep the night before last; I was driving."

"Oh, sorry, kiddo. Hey, why did you call me on that crappy cell phone yesterday and not this landline?"

"What landline?" Ella tried to focus on the conversation. She wanted to go back to sleep, but once woken, it would be impossible.

"The one you're talking on now, silly!"

Ella frowned and looked at what she was holding. Sure enough, it wasn't her disposable cell phone.

"Well, hell, imagine that." Ella chuckled. "So, how did you get the phone number? And, what is the phone number, by the way?"

"Amanda gave it to me."

"I don't imagine I should be making long distance calls on it."

"Amanda told me to tell you it was okay. I guess she checked with her brother and his plan has unlimited long distance, so you can go ahead and use it, as long as you aren't making international calls."

"Have you started your turkey?" Ella asked, remembering what day it was.

"No, not yet. Hey Ella, they were talking about you on the morning show. They say you're probably going to be on the New York Times Bestseller's list when this week's report comes out."

"Last night was the first time I've been online since before this fiasco. Connie, my sales are through the roof. You'll never believe how much money I've made this week. It's probably just a fluke, and when the story of me and Brady drops from the news, my numbers will go back to normal."

"Hey, Mom wants to talk to you. Hold on."

"Hi, honey. I am so proud of you! You're a best-selling author!"

"Thanks, Mom. It's all pretty crazy."

"Of course, your father is still upset about that picture on the Internet."

"I know, Mom. Me, too."

"When do we meet Brady, dear?"

"Mom, Brady and I aren't dating. I don't think you'll ever meet him."

"What's wrong, don't you like him? He seems like such a sweet boy, and he obviously adores you."

"What in the world are you talking about?"

Instead of an answer, Ella heard Connie snatch the phone from their mother.

"Ella," came Connie's voice, "I was getting ready to tell you. Brady was on a talk show last night. Look it up online; I bet the clip will be there. That's why I called Amanda; I wanted her take on this. Before you watch it, answer a serious question for me."

"What?"

"Are you in love with him?"

"That is none of your business," Ella snapped.

"Okay, baby sis. But maybe you need to ask yourself that question before you watch the video. Because I have a good hunch that cute guy is in love with you."

When Ella hung up the phone a few minutes later, she retrieved her laptop and turned it on. It took her only a few minutes to find Brady Gate's interview from the night before. Starting the video, Ella's heart gave a little lurch when she saw Brady sitting on the couch across from the show's host. Maybe he'd only been in her life a relatively short time, but walking away from him hurt far more than her breakup with Craig.

"You've survived an exciting adventure. Lost in a blizzard and rescued by a beautiful woman. But there's been some talk that all of this was some sort of publicity stunt."

"Publicity stunt? I hadn't heard that one." Brady laughed, yet Ella could tell by his body language, the question irritated him.

"This has definitely helped Ella Lewis's career."

"Ella is an extremely talented writer. I think it's wonderful readers have discovered her work. I'm only sorry it had to be done at the expense of her privacy. She didn't deserve any of that."

"You mean the photographs?"

"That and the paparazzi camping out at her cabin. Just because she rescued me in the middle of a blizzard and provided me a safe harbor, that is no reason for the press to invade the sanctity of her home."

"Oh, Brady, you know it's more than rescuing you. The pictures…."

"Any discussion regarding those photographs should be limited to how the photographer stepped across the line and broke laws. I understand that in my career choice, I've forfeited the right to privacy. Ella made no such bargain."

"It sounds like you care a great deal for her."

"That's an understatement. She's the only person I'd ever want to be snowbound with." The clip ended.

Ella wasn't sure how she felt about the video, or what it meant. If he cared so much, why hadn't he tried contacting her? After turning off the computer, she dressed in a pair of jeans and pullover sweater. She went to the kitchen and ate a bowl of cereal. Too restless to write, she turned on the television and did some channel surfing, but most of the programing was holiday related or reruns, and nothing captured her attention because she couldn't stop thinking of Brady.

Needing to clear her head, she decided to take a

walk along the ocean. For a moment, she considered taking Sam, but not sure dogs were permitted, she left her behind.

It took her just a few minutes to walk to the beach. When Ella reached the sand, she slipped off her shoes and held them while she walked along the water's edge. Only a few people shared the beach with her and they were some distance away.

Enjoying the solitude, she walked for about five minutes before sitting in the sand. She sat there for about twenty minutes, staring into the ocean and watching the breakers. Her solitude was interrupted when a shadow fell over her. Someone was standing behind her. Jerking her head up she turned around quickly to see who was standing so close in such an isolated area.

It was Brady. He stood, looking down at her, a quiet smile playing on his lips. Casually dressed in denims and a long-sleeved shirt, he looked relaxed.

"Brady," she whispered, not believing he was there. Her heart began to race and it took incredible willpower not to jump up and throw her arms around him.

"Hi, Ella, can I join you?" He sat down beside her before she could answer.

"How did you know where to find me?" She wondered if he could hear her heart beating. It sounded thunderous in her own ears. Taking a deep breath, she tried to stay calm.

"Your friend Amanda. You know, she can't keep secrets."

"Are you alone?" Ella asked, looking around, wondering who was watching them.

"I came alone. Although, that's not entirely true. Kevin and I drove to his sister's in Cayucos and she loaned me her car."

"You need to get your own car," Ella teased with a soft smile.

"You're probably right. I think I'm going to buy a house too. I'm a little tired of living in hotels." He glanced around then added, "A beach house would be nice."

"Why are you here, Brady?"

"I missed you. I understand you're a hot shot bestselling author now."

"I suppose I have you to thank for that."

"No, Ella, I've read the reviews. Readers love your books. In fact, my agent called. Apparently, you are impossible to contact, so agents and producers have been calling him, trying to get ahold of you. I understand there is serious interest in making several of your books into a mini-series for the History Channel. Sorry, Ella, but you're famous now. Maybe if you didn't have talent, all this would die down and you could slide back into anonymity."

"You don't think it will eventually die down?"

"Sorry, no. Even if I never see you again, you will

always have fans wanting a part of you. That's just part of the business."

Gazing out to the ocean, Ella silently considered his words.

"Here's the thing, Ella." Brady draped one arm around her. "I figure the privacy cat is pretty much out of the bag. You can't put that kitty back in there; he'll scratch your eyes out. So if that's the case, I see no reason for us not to be together."

"What?" Ella turned to look at him. In spite of the teasing tone in his voice, he looked utterly serious.

"I'm crazy about you, Ella Lewis. I think I'm in love with you."

Ella smiled; tears filled her eyes. She reached up and stroked the side of his face.

"I know I'm in love with you, Brady Gates."

CHAPTER EIGHTEEN

One Year Later

"This is amazing!" Amanda shifted the squirming baby from one hip to another as she looked out the enormous picture window and admired the stunning ocean view. She knew exactly what this prime piece of California real estate cost Brady and Ella, because they'd asked her to help them find a California real estate agent before they started shopping for a new home. The sweet referral commission she earned on the transaction enabled her and Chad to join family and friends for a Thanksgiving holiday along the coast while adding to their son's college fund.

"Here, let me take him," Ella offered, snatching the wiggly baby from Amanda. He went without protest and immediately started tugging on Ella's necklace while examining the diamond pendant attached to the gold chain.

The two women were alone in the living room. Sounds of a lively conversation drifted in from the kitchen area, reminding them it was a full house. Ella's last Thanksgiving would be remembered as her favorite, spending it alone with Brady at the Morro Bay beach house, dining on leftovers.

She was looking forward to this week, spending it in her new home with the people she loved most in the world. It had been an exciting and life-altering year, and she was looking forward to a peaceful holiday surrounded by close friends and family.

"I'm really glad you invited Chad and me up here for the week. Thanks again."

"You know you're always welcome. I do miss going up to the cabin, but that's not really possible these days. And I absolutely love this house."

"On the upside, it's been great for cabin rentals," Amanda said with a chuckle. "Yours is booked for the next nine months, and I never had people interested in winter rentals before."

"I had hoped the interest in Brady and me would have died down by now. I imagine it will eventually."

"At least you have this amazing new home. A gated community is probably the best option."

Gazing out at the panoramic ocean view, Ella silently agreed with her friend. She never intended to move in with Brady so soon, considering they had known each other such a short time. Miraculously, the press didn't discover her Morro Bay hideaway. When Brady wasn't in rehearsal or concert, he'd steal away to the borrowed beach house so they could spend time together.

In spite of the seclusion at Morro Bay, Ella's professional life was becoming more complicated. Keeping up with the flood of emails was becoming a fulltime job and she found it difficult to find the time to write. Even her personal life was getting strange. Suddenly forgotten classmates and cousins she hadn't heard from in years were contacting her mother, wanting to know how to reach the now famous Ella.

Thinking it might be easier to organize her life at her own home, Ella returned to the condo by the end of January. Unfortunately, the loss of her privacy continued to complicate her life. Strangers were showing up at her door, as well as the family members and old acquaintances who'd initially contacted her mother.

Brady was done with hotel living, and during that time, had decided to rent a beach house in a gated community. Knowing they would have no privacy at Ella's condo, it was decided they would get together at the beach rental. During Ella's first visit, Brady asked her to stay beyond the weekend. She only intended to stay a few extra days, but never went home. With Amanda's help, Ella's personal belongings were packed up and shipped to the beach house, and the condo sold.

Brady talked her into hiring a personal assistant, which helped organize her professional life. Through his connections, she signed with a reputable agent and sold her books' print rights to a major publishing house while retaining all her digital rights. Ella Lewis was a very rich woman.

"What are you two plotting?" Chad teased as he and Brady walked into the living room. Upon seeing his daddy, the baby in Ella's arms began to squirm. Chad quickly took his son from Ella and gave the boy a hug.

Brady stood next to Ella and wrapped one of his arms around her waist, pulling her tightly to him.

"You look good with a baby in your arms," Brady whispered, yet loud enough for his friends to hear.

"I heard that!" Amanda chimed. "I think you need to get married first."

"No one gets married anymore," Chad said as he bounced his baby boy in his arms.

"We're married!' Amanda reminded. Chad responded with a laugh.

"Should we tell them?" Brady asked slyly, giving Ella a little squeeze.

"I thought we were waiting for Thanksgiving dinner to make the announcement?" Ella scolded. "You just can't keep a secret!"

"Oh my god, you are getting married!" Amanda squealed.

"Not exactly." Brady chuckled.

"You're pregnant?" Amanda asked, looking Ella up and down for signs of an impending pregnancy.

"No I'm not pregnant!" Ella laughed. She shoved Brady with her hip, flashing him a mock scowl. Brady laughed, delighted at the guessing game.

"I can't marry this jerk," Ella told her friend.

"Why?" Amanda asked, wondering what the secret was.

"Because we're already married!" Ella laughed. "But don't say anything. We want to make the announcement during Thanksgiving grace, when we all share what we're thankful for."

"I don't understand. When did you get married? Why wasn't I invited?" Amanda asked.

"Don't be mad at us Amanda," Brady told her. "But considering the way we've been hounded by the press, we decided we wanted our wedding day to be completely out of the limelight. We felt the only way to do that was to elope."

"Do your parents know? Your sister?"

"Not yet, but considering those photos of me and Brady on the Internet, my father will be relieved."

They all laughed. Ella thought it felt wonderful to laugh at something that last year was so excruciatingly embarrassing. The four chatted for a few minutes longer before the baby started fussing.

Amanda and Chad left the room with their son, leaving the secret newlyweds alone.

"You really can't keep a secret," Ella teased, leaning into Brady.

"Funny thing, Ella, this is one secret I want to shout to the world. I'm just so damn happy."

Ella couldn't suppress her smile. "Let's go tell the others," she suggested.

Brady pulled her closer for a kiss. They wouldn't wait for Thanksgiving dinner to share their news. But it could wait until after the kiss.

Where readers first met Ella
Sundered Hearts

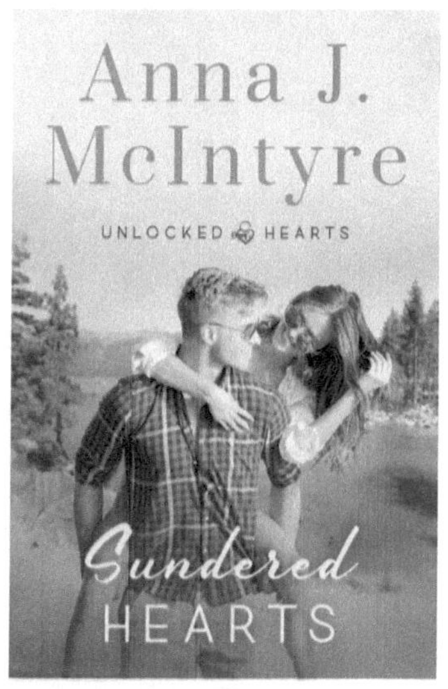

Susan Thomas thought she had it all—a home, a husband she loved, and children in her future—until everything came crashing down one rainy afternoon, exposing her perfect world as a lie.

Determined to move on with her life, Susan recklessly drags Brandon Carpenter from the bar and into her bed. When she doesn't see him again, Susan fears she is repeating her same old mistakes.

Seeking refuge at Shipley Mountain, the last

person Susan expects to run into is Brandon. He has his own reasons for being on the mountain. Brandon and Susan must put aside their misunderstandings. A child's life is at stake.

After Sundown

Women don't come to After Sundown for the beer – they come to get laid. When wealthy Cole Taylor walks into the bar that night, it's for a drink. He gave up one-night stands in his wild youth, but that changes when he sees her. She is too tempting to pass up, and by the looks from the other men at the bar, he needs to move quick to claim the prize.

Kit Landon - a struggling young widow, raising her daughter alone - has her own reasons for being at After Sundown. And it has nothing to do with illicit sex. But things can escalate a little too fast after nervously downing several beers on an empty stomach.

The conservative young widow finds herself in an

extremely compromising situation and barely manages to escape, leaving behind a furious Cole Taylor.

Kit never wants to see the man again, but she is in for a big surprise.

Sugar Rush

When Lexi Beaumont refuses to marry the man of her grandfather's choosing she is banished from her home and stripped of all her belongings. Being abandoned by the manipulative and selfish man who raised her is not especially traumatic – she's been looking for a way to leave her grandfather's home and was grateful for the college education he provided.

What she wasn't prepared for was her grandfather's attempt to sabotage her efforts at finding a job, nor did she realize he'd hired a man to spy on her.

Needing to regroup, Lexi and her best friend flee to Lake Havasu City, Arizona, to stay in her friend's vacation home. There she discovers a sweet path to financial security, with the help of the supportive and handsome neighbor, who is also new to Havasu. What she doesn't know, he's been hired by her grandfather.

HAUNTING DANIELLE

The Ghost of Marlow House

The Ghost Who Loved Diamonds

The Ghost Who Wasn't

The Ghost Who Wanted Revenge

The Ghost of Halloween Past

The Ghost Who Came for Christmas

The Ghost of Valentine Past

The Ghost from the Sea

The Ghost and the Mystery Writer

The Ghost and the Muse

The Ghost Who Stayed Home

The Ghost and the Leprechaun

The Ghost Who Lied

The Ghost and the Bride

The Ghost and Little Marie

The Ghost and the Doppelganger

The Ghost of Second Chances

The Ghost Who Dream Hopped